Sishma

Mohammadreza Riazi

Serial Number: P2236260113
Title: SISHMA
Sub Tittle: The Legend of Sishma
Author: Mohammadreza Riazi
Editor: Loretta Green
Translator: K.P.H. Group
ISBN: 978-1-990760-68-6
Metadata: Historcal Fiction
Cover Design: Mahboobeh Laalpoor
Book: Paperback
Pages: 218
Canada Publish Date: January 2023
Publisher: Kidsocado Publishing House

Kidsocado Publishing House
Vancouver, Canada

Phone : +1 (833) 633 8654
WhatsApp: +1 (236) 333 7248
Email: info@kidsocado.com
https://kidsocadopublishinghouse.com
https://kphclub.com

Attention:

Authors, and publishers rely on revenue from sales of this book to contribute to their livelihood. Photocopy and share the contents of this publication deprives the creators of their due compensation. For this reason, the material in this publication is protected by Copyright law. Please follow the intention of the law and do not photocopy. Reproduction of any part of this book without permission of publisher may lead to prosecution.

Author: Mohammadreza Riazi
Published by: KPH
Cover Design: KPH Design

©Copyright 2023 US Copyright

It is dedicated to my beloved wife,

Zohreh Heydari,

and my dearest daughters,

Saeedeh (Mina) and Sepideh (Mobina),

who were my main motivation for creating this work.

Preface

I sincerely appreciate my honorable masters: Esmaeel Rahbari, Abdullah Panahi, Ali Khosravi, Ehsan Ghafari, Alireza Neysari, and Ruholah Ghasemi, as well as all the dear ones of the Literary Association of Firoozabad Fars, who were guides and pioneers.

It should be noted that all historical events told in the story are derived from social media research, especially Persian Wikipedia, and it is accompanied by the author's speculation and popular quotes from Firoozabad Fars[1], although vague points; therefore, I have no claims regarding the rejection or acceptance of current historical information.

---

[1] Firuzabad is a city and capital of Firuzabad County, Fars Province, Iran. At the 2006 census, its population was 58,210, in 12,888 families. Firuzabad is located south of Shiraz. The city is surrounded by a mud wall and ditch.

(Wikipedia)

The Legend of Sishma

When P300 opened his eyes, he saw himself on a big hill that extended from both sides and was gently drawn to one side. When he looked more carefully, the hill seemed to meet again somewhere far away and formed a big circle of dirt. Among the heights and lowlands covered with flat plants, there were different parts without plants and a high earthen mass that stood right in the middle of this circle, similar to a tall and headless tree trunk. He looked behind himself. There was a landscape covered with plants that were irregularly divided into various shapes. The other side looked like black lines on which something was moving, and then the ground was drawn towards the sky. On one side, a little further from where he stood, multifarious volumes could be seen in a relatively vast gamut. He did not know anything about his surroundings.

P300:

- Dear leaf, where am I? There is no human here.

Sishma leaf:

- As far as I know, the gate of Hormuz, Gour[1] City, is under your feet.

---

[1] The ancient city of Gour is located 3 kilometers from the current city of Firozabad. It was the first circular city in Iran and one of the first circular cities in the world, which was built by the order of Ardeshir Babkan. It has four main gates, namely Hormuz Gate in the north, Ardeshir Gate in the south, Mehr (Mitra) Gate in the east and Bahram Gate in the west. (Wikipedia)

P300:

- Here, there are only plants that have no similarity with our Sishma or Savich bushes. There is nothing else but the hill on which I have stood.

Sishma leaf:

- My information is related to many years ago, so much the better if there is no one. As you have stood, you should go toward the right side. Look at me; from now on, instead of talking, just look at me. I will tell by this sign which direction you should go to find the uranium stone. It is better not to talk with me in front of people.

P300:

- Why?

Sishma leaf:

- It is dangerous for both of us.

P300 accepted the leaf's words and moved in the direction it was pointing to. A little later, he heard a voice. He looked and saw something moving. A creature similar to him sat on that moving thing which turn and break up soil. He asked the leaf, and the leaf said,

- The one that turns the earth upside down is the plow, and the one that moves is the chariot[1]. Maybe

---

[1]

humans have made a new device. As I said earlier, humans are powerful device creators.

After a few moments, Sishma leaf said,

- So, we will face the problem. Lie on your back somewhere on the short plants and put me on your forehead. Keep silent until I have said something.

P300 did this, and a few minutes later, Sishma leaf spoke again:

- Get up now. I have transferred to you whatever I knew. Hide the red seed and me somewhere so that no one sees us. Remember not to eat anything. Otherwise, you will be cursed by Ir. When your mission is done, come to us so we can return to Souch. From now on, any question you have, just put your hand on your forehead and keep silent for a moment, and you will know the answer.

P300 hid Sishma leaf somewhere and left a sign to find it again and continued moving. A few moments later, he heard a voice that seemed to be slowly coming towards him. A creature with sharp teeth was sounding, and something was moving behind him. He was a little scared and stopped immediately. He put his hand on his forehead and kept silent for a moment. He smiled and said to himself, It is so interesting that a harmless animal called a dog is satisfied with pieces of bread or bones, fawns its tail, barks, and watches over humans like this.

Later, he got familiar with chickens, roosters, donkeys, cows, horses, and other domestic animals. Sometimes, he imitated their voices like children and mostly enjoyed the response of the turkeys.

A moaning sound was coming from behind, getting louder and closer every moment. He stopped and looked behind himself timidly and hesitantly. He saw something on which two people sat, and it was coming towards him from a distance. He immediately put his hands on his forehead and kept silent; he could not find a better answer than the new chariot. He decided to figure out its name with a wise question. *But what should I ask?* he thought. He decided to show himself as an oblivious one when the sound approached him. Two individuals who had sat on it raised their hands, and he did so. Slightly ahead, the new chariot stood. The one who had sat behind turned towards him and asked,

- What are you doing with such a look?

Without waiting for his answer, he continued.

- Are you lost? It's a pity that our engine is not strong enough for more than two people. Otherwise, we would have taken you to the village.

P300 waved. The chariots moaned, and gradually, they moved away. P300 stared at them for a few moments, and the soil that had been raised behind them played with his mind. A little later, he sat on a rock, put his hand under his chin and thought. Through this brief encounter with two humans, he realized his appearance was different from others, and he had landed in an unknown world. The fear of the unknown caused him to think about eating a red seed and returning to Souch planet. But he regretted so soon, more than anything, his inability to save the Souch planet and the sense of shame before others caused him to rethink leaving. He decided to face his fears and finish his mission. He must change his appearance before others at the first opportunity. But how? He hesitated slightly, and after saying, *Ir help me,* started walking. While walking towards the village, he expressed his thoughts, hoping for the aid of Ir. Talking to himself, *I will find a proper way. It is better to become an oblivious one. I will find a way, yes, a way. I will find a proper way, he said.*

As soon as he reached the village, he felt the heavy looks of others. It didn't take long before the crowd besieged him, and everyone had questions.

- Who are you?
- What are you doing here? Are you lost?
- Have you filmed?
- What historical period does this dress belong to?
- I know. I have seen it in Sar Be Daran. It is related to the period of the Mongols, am I right?

Similarly, they asked incessantly, and some told others their guesses.

The best solution for P300 was silence and just silence, sometimes nodding as a sign of approval. In his heart, he wanted Ir to help him. He reached the peak of confusion and helplessness. A voice came, different from others in his surroundings. The resonance of the voice calmed his heart. The voice came closer, and its face was the same as P301. He was almost about to hug him and say aloud, "P301, you saved me," but he controlled himself for a moment and remained silent. Then, the person behind the voice said,

- The guest is God's friend[1]. Let's go to the house and take a rest.

P300 smiled and nodded as a sign of appreciation and followed him. After opening something he had never seen, the stranger passed through a wall and said,

- Please, come in. No one is in the house. Take it easy; we men are more comfortable with loneliness.

P300 followed him and passed through the wall, and he saw trees in front of himself. He sat in a corner on a flat similar to P365's. After closing the door, the stranger came toward him and said,

- I closed the door of the yard so you wouldn't be bothered by anyone. The yard not comfortable. Come inside.

P300:

- It's very good. I won't come into the room. I will rest here for a short time.

Man:

- As you wish. I will be back. Then he went to the room.

P300 said to himself, *"So its name is the door of the yard."* Then when he saw the trees in the yard, he put his hand on his forehead and was silent for a moment. He started to name them: *"tangerine, orange, sweet lime, lemon."* It didn't take long before the man came with something in his hand and said,

---

[1] An expression in Persian language that shows the important of the guests.

-   Come on, I have brought freshly-made tea, an excellent one.

P300 moved his hand as a sign of unwillingness and said,
-   I don't want to eat anything.

Man:
-   It is okay to try it. I won't ask anything in exchange.

P300:
-   No, I don't eat anything at all.

He wanted to say that if he ate, he would be cursed by Ir, but he kept silent.

Man:
-   It is not Ramadan. Are you fasting?

P300 put his hand on his forehead and remained silent for a moment.
-   Yes, I am fasting.

Man:
-   What a pity. Do you want to take a shower?

P300:
-   No, thanks.

Man:
-   Do you need any help? Can I help you?

P300 thought a little and then moved his cloth with his finger. The man smiled and said,

- Oh, I get it, you want some clothing. Hold on.

Then he went in and returned with different clothes. P300 eyed the clothes and then chose one among them.

Man:
- This one is so good. It suits your look as well. Come in and change your cloth.

P300:
- No, let me change it right here, behind this orange tree.

Then he got up immediately.

The man glanced at P300 shockingly and said,
- As you wish.

As he was changing his clothes, the man said,
- You didn't tell me what the filming is about.

P300 put his hand on his forehead and answered,
- It is the story of a man who came from many years ago and is now looking for the ur-an-nim stone he had hidden in a hollow many years ago.

Man:
- Do you mean the uranium stone?

P300 put his hand on his forehead and answered.
- Yes.

After changing clothes, P300 folded his old clothes neatly, went towards the man, handed them to him, and said,

- You did a favor for me. Please accept these clothes from me as a trust. I will be back soon, and I will make this love up somehow. See you soon and bye.

Then he went towards the door of the yard, and after fiddling with the door lock for a while, he opened it and went outside.

The man, witnessing P300's words and behavior shockingly, raised his hand slowly and said in a low voice,

- Bye.

After leaving, P300 continued on his way. The unknowns of his surroundings were so much that he put his hand on his forehead many times. He did not understand, and these situations bothered him from the inside. The askance look by the people around him dissatisfied him. He walked on a dirt path and then on a black path and looked around shockingly until, finally, he stopped at the threshold of a courtyard door. He pushed the door a little; it was closed. He put his hand on his forehead and kept silent for a moment. He was looking for something on the door until he knocked on it, but he didn't find anything. He looked around, picked up a stone, and knocked on the door. He knocked on the door again for a moment, and four small stars beside the door lit up. A voice reached for P300's ears.

- Who are you looking for?"

P300 looked at the small stars at first timidly and shockingly and then looked around.

Voice:

- Are you out of your mind? I said who are you looking for?

He looked at the small stars again and said hesitantly with a trembling voice,

- Uranium.

Voice:

- What? Who?

P300:

- Uranium.

Voice:

- Let it go. You're not making any sense.

After a while, the little stars went out.

P300 knocked on the door many times and talked with a voice coming from beside the small stars, but he did not reach his goal of getting the uranium stone.

A few hours passed in this way. P300 was leaning on the door meekly, stemming from his helplessness, when someone similar to a teenager on his planet, with something strapped to his back, approached.

She asked,

- Pardon me, who are you looking for?

P300:

- Uranium.

Girl:

-   Who?

P300:

-   I told you, Uranium.

Girl:

-   We don't have a person or anything called by such a
    name here.

P300:

-   Let me see if I understood correctly. Do you also live
    in this cave?

She laughed and said,

-   People don't live in caves for a long time. You should
    be a witty person. Anyway, this cave you talk about
    is me and my mother's house.

P300:

-   I am not a human to be able to joke. So, you call your
    cave a house? What does mother mean?

She laughed and said,

-   So, you don't know the meaning of mother?

She laughed again and continued,

-   Mom, mommy. naneh, mother. Got it?

P300:

-   Wait a moment (he put his hand on his forehead and
    kept silent). I got it. A creature that gives birth to a

child is called a mother by humans. So interesting. It means that people live along with their mother's ashes?

Girl:

- What are you saying to yourself? We are not Buddhists. My mother has not died at all.

P300:

- Interesting. It means that your mother is alive? Does she breathe? Do you see her?

Girl:

- Why not? She kisses me several times a day; before school, after school, before sleep, and after sleep.

P300:

- Kiss?

Girl:

- You mean you don't know this either? What is a kiss? The pressure of the two lips. See, this is called a kiss (then she imitates how to kiss).

P300:

- Well, so what?

Girl:

- When someone kisses you, you will feel good.

P300:

- It means if you kiss me, I will feel good? You know, I miss the Souch.

Girl:

- I mustn't kiss you. I must fall in love with you before I can. When you see Souch, tell it to kiss you.

P300:

- Souch has not a lip. Anyway, tell me, what should I do for you to love me?

Girl:

- When the appropriate time comes, someone will fall in love with you.

P300:

- When does it take place?

Girl:

- I don't know. Maybe in two, five, or even ten years.

P300:

- I won't be here in two years. Maybe I would even be a child.

Girl:

- What do you say to yourself? Why do you even want to be a child? Anyway, you are very strange. Who are you anyway? What are you doing here?

P300:

- My name is P300. I will begin to burn after 730 days and then turn into light, like the other Ps that became light the night I survived. When that morning approaches, my ash becomes one new P300. Then I will become a child and work along with the elders to grow again.

Girl:

- 730 days? One year?

P300:

- Yes, one year in the Souch planet of the Ir system from the Ann galaxy means one year.

Girl:

- Ir? Ann?

P300:

- What I said is our galaxy. Ir is also the name of our star. We love it so much, and in the morning, when we come out of the cave, we lie on our chest ten times and get up again. Anyway, it also loves us so much.

Girl:

- How did you understand?

P300:

- It comes at the end of every day to give us life. The Sishma tree says that Ir has made all Ps and Zs as well.

Girl:

- What are you talking about? Who are Ps and Zs?

P300:

- P creatures are all like me, and Zs are similar to you. Of course, a little older than you. They live in the left half of the Souch planet.

Girl:

- Well, say it clearly, men and women?

P300:

- How many times do I repeat it? I said that I am not a human.

Girl:

- You mean that in the place where you came from, the Ps and the Zs do not stay with each other?

P300:

- Of course not. What do we have to do with each other? We are on the right side, they are on the left side, and there is a high wall separating us.

Girl:

- Does it mean you don't want to have a baby?

P300:

- How many times should I say? After 730 days, we burn for one year, and in the morning, we become children, and they celebrate Mehrgan for us. After one month, or 60 days, we grow up. Up to now, they celebrated me after respecting Ir to the extent of 384 times.

Girl:

- Never mind. You mean you've been burned 384 times and turned into a child? You mean that you come from another galaxy where men and women have nothing to do with each other? Is there a hidden camera? Where did you embed it?

P300:

- I don't know what a hidden camera is, but when I volunteered to travel to the earth to save the Souch planet, the Sishma tree gave me a leaf to answer my questions, be a guide for my Journey, and be able to speak your language.

As she is scared a little, she presses her finger on something next to the place where the little stars light up. A sound comes, and then the little stars light up.

Girl:

- Mom, mom, come and see, what does he say?

Mom:

- Don't be afraid, my daughter. He is harmless and has told me many things in a few hours. Most importantly, he says that he is going to look for the uranium stone that is in our house.

Girl:

- Well, you could have told him to take it inside.

Mom:

- After all, I was alone. I phoned your uncle Farhad. He will come soon.

P300:

- So, she is a girl. phone? Uncle?......

Girl:

- Why don't you come inside?

P300:

- If you light a fire in your cave, excuse me, your house, I will come inside.

Girl:

- Why?

P300:

- To light up everywhere.

Meanwhile, someone arrives.

Girl:

- Hi, uncle.

Uncle:

- Hi, naughty girl. I see you are busy with science studies this summer. What's going on with the club?

Girl:

- Nothing, as usual.

Mom:

- Hi, dear brother! Long time no see! Finally, you came!

Uncle:

- I swear by God that I was busy, my dear Fariba. Is this the same idiot you were talking about? Didn't you call the police?

Fariba:

- He has been driving me crazy for two or three hours. I called, but they still haven't come.

P300:

- Uncle? Club? Idiot? Police?

Girl:

- (harassingly) How many times would you ask? Come inside, and I will tell you.

P300:

- No, I'm not coming. It's dark.

Girl:

- (laughs) You are grown up but are still afraid of the dark?

P300:

- You asked why I am scared of that. We are alive by the light.

Girl:

-   (Laughs again) Well, don't worry; come inside. We have little stars in our cave that light up everywhere.

P300:

-   Small stars?

Girl:

-   Come in, so I can explain to you.

Uncle:

-   Who is this fellow? And why have you asked him to come in? Everyone cannot come into the house.

P300:

-   Fellow? (He put his hand on his forehead and kept silent.) The curse word?

Uncle:

-   Fellow is not a curse word. If there is a need, I will use it so you do not disturb anyone.

P300:

-   I did not disturb.

Uncle:

-   So, what the hell were you doing during these two hours?

As P300 was listening to the uncle's words, he saw a chariot on which two small red stars flashed approaching them.

After that, the hubbub was heard.

- Excuse me. They were good neighbors. What did they do?
- Please go and don't disturb.
- Ladies and gentlemen, please leave here and don't gather.
- Lady, what are you filming? Turn off your phones. Didn't I ask you to leave here? Go, or we will arrest you too.

P 300:
- I had nothing to do with them. I just came to take the uranium stone.

Police officer:
- Sir, it seems to be a serious security issue.

Voice from walkie talkie:
- Transfer everything to the center by consideration of observing all security cases.

Police officer:
- Yes, sir.

Fariba:
- What kind of police emergency service is this? We called you.

Girl:

- What are you doing to my mother?

Police officer:

- Do not make noise, naughty girl. You should come as well. Get in immediately.

Uncle:

- Hey, douchebag, don't you have any honor? Why do you treat her like this?

Police officer:

- Zip it. Get in immediately. Just wait, then you will realize who the ignorant man is.

Voice from walkie talkie:

- Check each part of the house and make sure that there is no one else, then seal off the house.

Then, P300, along with others, was forcibly put in the chariot and taken away.

✳✳✳✳✳✳

Male interrogator:

- Specification; first name and family name?

P300:

- P300.

Male interrogator:

- What did you say?

P300:

- P300.

Male interrogator:
- The offspring of?

P300:

- P300.

Male interrogator:
- It seems you don't realize this is where roosters hatch.

P300:

- Roosters cannot hatch.

Male interrogator:
- But here is where they hatch.

******

Female interrogator:

Specification:
- first name and family name?

Fariba:

- Fariba Heydari.

Female interrogator:
- The offspring of?

Fariba:

- Ghasem. Anyway, why am I here? Where is my daughter?

******

Male interrogator:

- Specification; first name and family name?

Uncle:

- Farhad Heydari.

Male interrogator:

- The offspring of?

Uncle:

- Ghasem.

******

Female interrogator:

- Specification: first name and family name?

Girl:

- (Timid and crying) Mobina.

Female interrogator:

- Do you think this is a kindergarten? Introduce yourself properly.

Mobina (girl):

- (Timid and crying) Mobina Riazi.

Female interrogator:
- The offspring of?

Mobina (girl):
- (Timid and crying) Reza, Mohammadreza.

******

P300:
- It is the hen that hatches.

Male interrogator:
- Tell me the truth; in which secret service do you work?

P300:
- Secret service? Work? I don't know what your words mean.

Male interrogator:
- In which country do you work as a secret agent?

P300:
- Secret agent? Country?

Male interrogator:
- Why do you play innocent? Do you think you will be saved by this scenario?

P300:
- Scenario? Oh, Ir, help me, what do they say? Who did you mistake me for?

Male interrogator:

- Now you are talking. Who is Ir? Where is he hidden? What is the connection to him? What is your code?

P300:

- Connection? Code? What do your words mean?

Male interrogator (laughs):

- Playing innocent is a courageous but foolish move.

******

Female interrogator:

- Tell me, who is Ir?

Mobina:

- (Crying) That man said that Ir is the name of the system he came from.

Female interrogator:

- Who was that man?

Mobina:

- He said 300. Errr…..! P300.

******

Female interrogator:

- So, you believe such nonsense.

Fariba:

- What can I say? I told you what I heard.

Female interrogator:

- It seems you don't realize you have a role in a heavy case.

Fariba stared at the interrogator and shed tears.

******

Farhad:

- Yes, I have heard. They say that they hatch here.

Male interrogator:

- So, stop beating about the bush and say whatever you know.

Farhad:

- What should I say? I just saw this fellow a few minutes ago.

******

P300:

- Souch planet of Ir system, from Ann Galaxy, with a high wall divided into two parts with equal conditions. The only difference is its residents. In each half, there are 730 people whose food is light and air. They only go to their cave to be secured from the rain at night; each night, one person is burnt calmly, silently without raising any smoke, and he will be turned into light for everyone to survive. His ash will be turned into a child in the morning that grows up after one month or 60 days and, like the others born in the cave, lives for 730 days or one year.

******

Female interrogator:
- Who are Ps and Zs?

Mobina:
- According to his words, Ps are men and Zs are women, and there is a high wall between them. He said that he has been burnt 384 times and turned into a child while the others celebrated him.

******

P300:

- When we come out of the cave every morning, we see the Ir and lie down on our chest ten times in respect for Ir. Sishma told us that Ir has made us and helps us forever. We celebrate Ps who are born by grinding and crushing the branches of the Savich, which we have already picked a few days before then we drop them beside the Savich bush. We trim the branches; that's why our air is provided by them, and we protect them.

******

Female interrogator:
-   Who is Sishma?

Girl:

-   He didn't tell me about it. Why don't you ask him?

******

P300:

-   Our ancestors had told us that we should not eat the
    Sishma leaf as we would catch the incurable disease.
    But one day in the morning, P365 came out of the
    cave to get some fresh air, and when the Sishma tree
    had slept, he picked a leaf of the tree as he was
    feeling hungry and ate the Savich. It resulted in him
    becoming so strong that he no longer needed the
    light. He ate the Savich all the time and defecated
    everywhere; the whole environment was covered
    with a strong stench. He even made a bench from the
    Savich's wood next to the cave and didn't let anyone
    enter the cave unless they had a fresh leaf of the
    Savich. At night, he violated the recent matures, and
    some of them served him. Recently, he had decided
    to destroy the high wall, possess Zs, and rule the
    whole planet. We were tired. Do you understand
    what I am saying?

******

Mobina:

- He didn't tell anything about P365. I am tired. When do I see my mother?

******

Male interrogator:

- You want to say all of you, decided that one of you all should eat the Sishma leaf and get even with P365?

He laughed and continued.

- Gosh!

P300:

- P31 asked P730 to eat the leaf since it was his turn to burn that night, and after celebrating his burning, the matter would end happily. We liked this new thought, and in the evening, we picked up a leaf when the Sishma had slept, and P730 ate. A few moments later, we all realized what we had done was wrong. Now, P730 didn't intend to burn for others; he wanted to eat the fresh leaves of the Savich and become powerful enough to become the ruler of Souch's Ps instead of P365 or go to the other side of the wall and become the ruler of Zs.

****

Male interrogator:

- You should know Sishma?

Farhad:

- What the hell is Sishma? Oh God, in what language should I speak? I was in my butcher's shop when my sister called and said an idiot knocked and said he came from another planet. I decided to see for myself what he was talking about. I left. It took a while. I wasn't even there for four or five minutes when your agents arrived, and I am still at your service. I don't know about anything at all.

******

P300:

- That night in the cave, P729 was burned. The next night, when the Sishma tree opened its eyes, it saw that we all surrounded it. At first, it was afraid and shielded its branches, but P728 shouted, *"We have not come to steal leaves, but we have come for consultation and help; there is a big problem that we hope you know how to solve."* The tree branches returned to their normal position, smiled, and asked, *"Is this problem not related to my lost leaf?"* Then it glanced at itself and yelled, *"Oh Ir, please, help me and send the wind to ask if it has delivered my leaf to the planetary prince."* P728 answered, *"There is no need to call the wind. We have picked the leaf for P730."* Then he narrated all the events to the tree.

******

Female interrogator:
- P31, P728, P729, P730, who are they, and how do you communicate with them?

Mobina:
- Oh God, it's enough. I'm tired. I want my mother.

******

P300:
- Sishma sighed and said, *"Ir forgive me for trying in vain to accuse wind of stealing at night. I will apologize to him as soon as it comes."* It sighed and continued again. *"One of you should go on a long Journey to planet Earth from the solar system in the Milky Way galaxy and bring 60 drops of uranium extract from there."* P728 said, *"We are unable to travel."* Sishma answered, *"Don't worry, I will give a green seed to go and a red seed to return to anyone who volunteers to travel, but he should know that he will be forgetful for the rest of his life a few days after his return. Going and returning of this Journey takes place in the blink of an eye; after reaching the ground, it takes time to stay there. Therefore, the age of the candidate must be between one month and six months."*

****

Mobina:

- He said when he volunteered to travel toward the earth to save the Souch planet, the Sishma leaf gave him a leaf to receive the answer to questions, be a guide during his travel, and talk to us in our language.

******

P300:

- I said, *"We will not survive without the light."* Sishma answered, *"These seeds provide light for your Journey, and as far as I know, the days of the earth are bright with a star called the sun, and humans, who are the powerful inhabitants of the earth, invented fire for their darkness, which makes their night light."* P300: I asked, *"How do you know these things?"* Sishma answered, *"A thousand years ago, when your ancestor, the great P300, the savior of Souch planet, returned before completely forgetting, he shared lots of memories about the earth and humans and then kept silent forever."* You know how interesting it is that my ancestor had been the saver of the Souch planet, and I didn't know? Sishma said they told this story from time to time for generations to the extent that its effect decreased, and people didn't speak about that.

******

Fariba:

- What I heard, I said to you. Don't you have any religion and faith? I want my daughter.

******

P300:

- Then P728 asked the tree to talk more about humans. Sishma answered: *"Humans have weak but huge bodies. They make devices through their thoughts. When they have good thoughts, it will result in food and calmness, but when they have bad thoughts, it results in war and killing."* P728 asked, *"Killing, war?"* Sishma said, *"I didn't understand these two correctly from the scattered words of the great P300. I just understood that a human or human beings take the lives of other beings or other human beings to destroy their life."* P728 asked, *"Does that mean people don't burn to survive others?"* Sishma said, *"Not the way you know; some people give their lives for other people or even trees and other creatures of nature."*

P300:

I asked, *"Does that mean they may destroy our life?"* Sishma said, *"Most of the wars are because of women, land, power, or the proof of an ideology. I don't know what that is, but you don't have any of them. I don't think you will be killed. Anyway, I told you that your Journey is long and dangerous."*

****

Female investigator:

- Who is P31?

Mobina:

- How do I know who he is? Ask yourself. I am tired.

******

P300:

- I asked the tree, *"Does it mean there is no hope for any human being?"* Sishma said *"Many people are kind and trying to reach peace and tranquility on earth. This talking leaf can be a guide to finding the uranium stone and also warn you of people who have bad thoughts by approaching them."*

P300:

I asked, *"How can the extract be obtained from uranium stone?"* Sishma said, *"This leaf answers all the questions."* I said, *"If that is the case, I will accept this Journey to be the savior of the planet like my great-grandfather."* Everyone clapped for me, and I took the leaves and seeds amid the applause of others. I ate the green seed, and after a few moments, my eyes were closed for the first time in my life.

******

Farhad:

- How do I know these people that you are throwing at me like machine gun bullets? I said that I had arrived just a few minutes before you.

****

P300:

- When I opened my eyes, I was on a big hill. I lay down somewhere on the grass on my back and put a Sishma leaf on my forehead. It transferred everything it knew to me. Now, every time I put my hand on my forehead, it tells me what it knows.

Male investigator:

- So where is the leaf of Sishma and the red seed you are talking about?

P300:

- Sishma told me to hide them somewhere. Then I walked until I reached the door of that house, and now I am still here.

******

Female investigator:

- In these few days, we have checked the history of each of you. Even though your brother is mischievous, none of you has a bad history.

Fariba:

- Does this mean we can go? Does that mean I will finally see my daughter?

******

Farhad:

- Let's think that I have made two irreconcilable arguments. Don't look at my misleading figure. Behind this copper star, there is a heart of gold.

Male investigator:

- I said that our problem is not related to you three but.....

******

Fariba:

- Oh God, are you still making difficulties?

Female investigator:

- The guy who himself introduces himself as P300 and says came from outer space, but the DNA results show that he is from a nearby area.

Fariba:

- Well, what does this matter have to do with us?

******

Male investigator:

- This means you are still indicted for cooperation with the secret police.

Farhad:

- I hope you die, P300. As you have come, you have made difficulties now. How can we prove that we have no pretension, to begin with?

******

Mobina:

- So, you are saying that my mother and Uncle Farhad have promised to cooperate? Does it mean that P300 is going to come into our house under the name of my mother's guest or suitor or anything else so that you can find out who he is and where he came from?

******

Farhad:

- After all, this is not possible. It may take a month. Should I stay at my sister's house?

Male investigator:

- Do you want to stay here forever?

Farhad:

- (Annoyed) It seems that there is no other way. What should we do?

Male investigator:

- Before we release everyone, we will teach you three how to treat P300. Then you can decide what excuse you would use to lure him into the house.

Farhad:

- Does that mean we should bring home a stranger we know nothing about? It's dangerous.

Male investigator:

- There is no other way. The only remaining way is the plan of friendship. You have to make him speak in any possible way and find out who he is and where he came from.

Farhad:

- Why don't you ask yourself?

Male investigator:

- Since he was arrested; he has neither slept nor eaten anything; If he continues like this, he will die, and the mystery will remain unsolved. The integrity of the country is in danger.

******

Mobina:

- Does it mean it is dangerous?

Female interrogator:

- We still don't know. But don't worry, you are under close supervision, and your safety is our priority.

Mobina:

-   It is a difficult job.

Female interrogator:

-   The most difficult part of your work is that you should be brave, just like the soldiers who defend their country.

******

Fariba:

-   It means that you have embedded cameras and microphones everywhere, that is, we cannot change the clothes either?

Female interrogator:

-   Don't worry, the bedroom is clean. P300 must not enter there. The bathroom and toilet can only be used when necessary.

******

Inside the house

P300 looked inside the house astonishingly and explores the surroundings.

Farhad:

-   Why is he behaving like this?

Mobina:

-   I don't know, but he says he came from another planet.

Farhad:

- Is it possible? He looks like a human to a great extent! His face is also very similar to my deceased friend's.

Fariba:

- Oh, you're right. I keep telling myself I've seen him somewhere. He's just like Pirooz.

P300:

- Pirooz? Pirooz? Pirooz?

Fariba:

- I'll go get something. After all that has happened, we ought to eat something.

Farhad:

- Well, my dear, you didn't say anything about the science club.

Mobina:

- Nothing. Just the day before P300 came, we were researching the historical city of Firouzabad. The most interesting thing was that it was written on Wikipedia; Ardeshirkhore[1], Gour, Gour, or the ancient Firoozabad, in the 7th or 8th century of the Hijri, ruined for unknown reasons and became deserted. What do you think could be the reason?

---

[1] Ardashir-Khoareh was one of the four administrative divisions of the Sasanian province of Pars. The other administrative divisions were Shapur-hwarrah, Istakhr and Darabgerd, while a fifth named Arrajan was founded in the early 6th century by Kavad.

P300:

- Ardeshirkhoreh! Ardeshir! Ardeshir! Ardashir! Gour! Gour! Gour!

(He puts his hand on his forehead, and the voice of the leaf in his head says, "P300, take the stone soon before it's too late.)

Farhad:

- Why is he behaving like this?

Mobina:

- Didn't you hear? I asked him on the way, and he said he was talking to his Journey guide.

Farhad:

- The same Sishma leaf that he said he had hidden somewhere?

Mobina:

- Yes, dear uncle. So, you have heard too?

Farhad:

- My dear! This can be considered an amazing subject for a live on Instagram.

As soon as Farhad turned on his phone, P300 went to him, took the phone and said,

- How interesting is it that your leaf is giving you light?

Farhad took the phone back, turned it off, and put it in his pocket, saying,

-    I want nothing to do with this. I have paid a great sum of money for this and I will not have you burn it to ground.

Fariba came with a serving tray of juice, put it on the table, and said,

-    This is fresh homemade apple juice. Drink it, I make you fresh.

P300:

-    Does that mean if I drink it, I will be enlightened? I will not drink it anything.

Farhad:

-    I'm starting to get bored step by step. Have you seen yourself at all? Get me a mirror.

Fariba took a mirror out of her bag and gave it to Farhad.

Farhad:

-    Come and see yourself.

P300, after a complete examination of the mirror, said,

-    Does this mean it's me?

Farhad:

-    You see, you are not that different from me. That means, whatever I can eat, you can eat. You should eat like a human, or we forcefully pour it into your throat so that you can understand that we are not different.

Fariba:

-   What are you doing? Don't bother him. He doesn't like to eat.

Farhad:

-   I am serving him so that he can get out of the illusion of being a spaceman, take it, and eat.

P300 moved his hand fearfully and hesitantly toward the glass and said,

-   No, I will not drink. If I do, I will be cursed by the Ir.

Farhad got up, held the glass of juice before P300's mouth, and said,

-   If you don't drink, you will be cursed by me

He poured the drops of the apple juice into P300's mouth. P300 started drinking forcefully. After one or two drops of water poured down P300's throat, Farhad sat down, put the glass on the table, and with a smile from success, said,

-   Are you still on a hunger strike? In the detention center, the task would have been completed if they had entrusted you to me from the very first day.

Fariba shook Farhad in such a way as not to draw the attention of P300 but to make Farhad understand that he was sabotaging. Farhad came to his senses and did not continue.

P300 looked around with surprise and got up, raising his hand toward his head and saying,

- Where am I? What are these ugly clothes? How has it covered me? These pleasant lights that I see on the roof of the house are lit by which fire? Not a flame that dances with a little breeze, not a smoke that makes tears flow from my eyes through painful attacks and not the summer heat that is demanding for the body.

P300 opened his hands along his shoulders, spun, took a deep breath, and continued.
- And this pleasant and fragrant air.

P300's eyes turned toward the sofa. He went to it, put his hand on it, and sat down. He sighed loudly and continued.
- Artakhshatreh[1] didn't have a throne as magnificent as this. Really, where am I? Is this intense paradise or heaven?

Farhad:
- Good! Now, what's that supposed to mean? Who is he?

P300, as if he had just noticed the presence of others, got up and asked amazingly:

---

1 Artakhshatreh or Artaxerxes was the fifth King of Kings of the Achaemenid Empire, from 465 to December 424 B.C.

- Who are you?" (He put a hand under his chin and continued after a moment of hesitation) It is better to ask in this way; what am I doing here now.

Mobina:

- We came together from the detention center to our house to know each other better.

P300:

- Detention center?

Fariba:

- So, you forgot so soon that we were arrested and interrogated?

P300:

- Does that mean we have been in jail and be responsible for the prisoners and night watches?

Farhad:

- Oh, the trouble has just begun. I think we won't finish our work in a month.

P 300:

- Who is aware of this calamity that has occurred?

Mobina:

- Uncle Farhad does not mean this calamity you are talking about.

P300:

- Uncle

Fariba:

- Farhad, you should know my brother. Anyway, Farhad, did you say that Arash runs the store?

Farhad:

- So, it is now clear that my presence is important?

P300 asked mobina:

- So, my daughter, is Farhad your uncle? And you have another uncle named Arash? It's interesting.

Farhad:

- He will soon become friendly. Mobina is not your daughter. What is interesting?

P300:

- Mobina is a beautiful name. It means *"obvious and enlightening."* But what is interesting to me is the name of your other uncle, Arash.

Mobina:

- Thank you, it is very kind of you.

Fariba:

- Are you sure you want to say again what a beautiful name it is, Arash also is the name of the legend of Iran.

P300:

- Of course, there is no doubt that it is something to be proud of, but what was interesting to me before that was that he had the same name as my wife's brother.

Mobina:

- Brother? Wife?

Fariba:

- It means brother-in-law.

Farhad:

- Misfortune is exactly what you have brought us. At first, you were not a person, but now you have a brother-in-law.

P300:

- What kind of calamity have I landed you to deserve this curse? I am human, and my only sin is that I asked you what I am doing here. Of course, I did not hear an answer.

Mobina:

- Do you mean you forgot that you were looking for the uranium extract?

P300:

- Uranium? What is uranium?

Farhad:

- That's what I'm saying, a calamity, a calamity. Until now, you, name P300, were the savior of the Souch planet and were looking for the uranium stone.

P300:

- What is the Souch planet? Who is the other P300?

Fariba:

- He doesn't even know P300 anymore.

Mobina:

- P300 is you, you!

P300:

- P300? But my name is Pirooz. Is this intense heaven or paradise?

Farhad:

- Intense? Heaven? Paradise? Idiot, what are you saying?

Mobina:

- P300, Pirooz, or whoever you are, this is my house and my mom, Fariba.

Pirooz (P300):

- Mom? Fariba? Do you mean that your mother's name is Fariba?

Mobina:

- Yes, that's what I said.

Pirooz laughed and continued hesitantly:

- Did I hear exactly what you said? Did you call this palace, which I don't believe, a house? Many kings did not see this palace, even in their dreams. Where does this sweet and pleasant fragrance come from?

Fariba:

- I sprayed marigolds to get rid of the bad smell caused by the garbage left in the house.

Pirooz:

- Spray? Garbage? What are you saying?

While Mobina got up and went to the room, Farhad said:

- We are unlucky. The guard interrogated us because of P300. Now, it's his turn.

Fariba:

- What is thrown out is called garbage. And spray... how do I explain this?

At the same time, Mobina entered with a spray in her hand and said,

- This is called a spray.

Then Pirooz pressed on the nozel a little, and out came the spray. Pirooz reacted. After a while, he took the spray and examined it.

Fariba:

- Well done, my smart daughter. I was wondering how to interpret it. You saved me.

Pirooz:

- What an interesting event. The extract of perfume comes out with pressure. What a great achievement.

I will take it to Gour City, and I will understand how it works.

Mobina:

- Where is the Gour city?

Pirooz:

- It is a city in the state of Pars, in the middle of Bishapoor and Istakhar, the city where I come from.

Mobina:

- But the Gour City has been destroyed for years.

Pirooz:

- Woe to me. Did the wicked Mongols destroy the city?

Mobina:

- It is not known. Maybe it is the same. It was written on Wikipedia that Gour, Gur or ancient Firuzabad in the seventh or eighth century of the Hijri, for unknown reasons, fell into ruin and became deserted.

Pirooz:

- Ancient Firoozabad? Where is Firozabad?

Farhad:

- P300 or Pirooz, I am fed up with you! Do you think that you are in Shiraz now? Tabriz? Or maybe in Tehran? This hell that you are in is a house in Firoozabad.

Pirooz:

- What are these things you said? Were they all cities? I have not heard their name until now. Let's see if I understood correctly; you mean that now, a city named Firoozabad has been built on the ruins of Gour?

Mobina:

- The ruins of Gour are a few kilometers away from Firoozabad.

Pirooz:

- How many kilometers? What is kilometer?

Fariba:

- It means distance.

Pirooz:

- Woe to me; Let me see what day of what year is it now?

Farhad:

- 14 of Tir , 1401 SH.

Pirooz:

- I don't understand what you meant. What type of chronograph is this?

Mobina looked at the date on her phone and said,

- 5 /dhu'l-hijja/ 1443 AH or July 5, 2022.

Pirooz calculated for a few moments and then says:

- How interesting is it that the solar chronograph of ancient Iran has been mixed with the lunar Hijri and another chronograph has been invented?

Mobina:
- Yes, the lunar year is exactly 10 days, 6 hours, and 11 seconds shorter than the solar year.

Pirooz calculated again.

Farhad:
- What are you calculating?

Pirooz:
- Just wait a little.

Then he started calculating again, and others looked at him amusingly.

After a few moments, Pirooz opened his mouth to speak.
- Yes, that's it! Monday, 16 Esfand, 633 SH, 19 Muharram ul-Haram, 653 AH, 7 March 1255 A.D. Woe to me, does that mean 768 years, 3 months, and 26 solar days have passed? So, where are my fellow travelers?

Mobina:
- Fellow travelers?

Pirooz:

- Yes. Ziba, Arash, and an adventurer from the city of Gour. They must be nearby now. I must hurry to look for them.

Farhad:

- Don't try in vain. No idiot person has been seen nearby but you. Otherwise, they would have been arrested by now, and we would have been saved.

Fariba:

- From what? 768 years have passed?

Pirooz:

- Since Ziba, Arash, and an adventurer from the city of Gour are my fellow travelers, I must find them as soon as possible. I was their confidant.

Farhad raised the glass of apple juice, and after looking at it in amazement, he took a closer look after smelling it, and he said,

- No, it does not contain alcohol.

Pirooz took the glass, and after examining it, he said,

- Are you a doctor who knows alcohol and Zakaria Razi? What kind of potion is this?

Fariba:

- It's not a potion. It's just homemade apple juice.

Pirouz:

- I don't understand. Do you mean apple extract or, for example, an apple distillate?

Fariba:

- Drink a little, and you will know.

Pirooz drank a little and said,

- How interesting is it that people distill apples instead of sesame these days and make this pleasant taste?

Mobina:

- We have a device called a juicer with which we juice apples, carrots, and other things.

Pirooz:

- Is this machine a new type of device, and do you have it at home?

Mobina:

- Yes.

Pirooz:

- Are you one of the rich people in the city who own such a house or this device?

Mobina:

- Most of the people in the city have these houses and equipment.

Pirouz:

- (Happily) Does this mean that people have reached my long-standing wish? Now they don't need anything, and there is no news of war?

Fariba:
- I don't know about the needs of people, but there is a lot of war, and thousands and thousands of people are killed quickly by pressing a button.

Pirooz laughed, and at the same time, Farhad took the remaining glass of apple juice from Pirooz's hand and said:
- Don't drink more than this. I'm afraid you'll go back to B.C. Since you drank two sips, you've gone back about eight hundred years, meaning you go back four hundred years with each sip.

He laughed and continued.
- If you drink the whole of the pitcher, you should probably arrive at Noah's ark.

Pirooz:
- Indeed, I must find a way to my fellow travelers, but how?

Pirooz got up and looked for a way to find his fellow travelers immediately.

Fariba:
- Calm down a bit. Sit and think a little. Tell us more about yourself, and maybe we will conclude.

Pirooz:
- What can I say about myself?

Farhad:
- Start from your childhood to this point.

Pirooz:

- If I were to start from my childhood, it would take days and years.

Farhad:

- Did you live to the extent of Noah's life?

Pirooz calculated for a few minutes and then said:

- Now, 1843 years, two months and 20 solar days have passed since the date of my birth.

Farhad:

- Didn't I say it? Drink a few more pitchers of apple juice, and you will reach the age of dinosaurs.

Then he laughed and continued.

- I promise he either turned into an idiot or is pulling our legs.

Mobina:

- Uncle Farhad, even if what you say is true; we will benefit from hearing it. Just imagine you are watching a movie.

Fariba laughed and asked:

- When and where were you born exactly?

Pirooz calculated for some time, then said:

- To better understand me, I will give the date. April 15, 179 A.D., I was born somewhere around Istakhar[1].

Farhad:

- Enough, we are tired. Don't take us for idiots.

Mobina:

- Dear Uncle, wait and see what happens in the end. It is somehow interesting. It is like a movie.

Then she turned toward Pirooz and said,

- There is no problem. We will listen no matter how long it takes.

Pirooz:

- What is a movie? This is the consequence of the kind of mistake that has prevented me from receiving knowledge for 768 years, 3 months, and 26 solar days, and now to be drowned in horrible expanses of unknowns. Everything I see or hear here mocks my ignorance; despite the books I had read. I was the wisest person of my time. Because I am a needy child who needs education, how many books should I read to make up for my backwardness? If I sacrifice my life for this sorrow, would it be permissible? That is also impossible.

---

[1] Istakhr was an ancient city in Fars province, five kilometres (three miles) north of Persepolis in southwestern Iran.

Mobina:

- Don't worry; I will teach you a way to get any book you want or the answer to any question. In the blink of an eye, it will be prepared for you, but on the condition that you tell your story in a detailed way, I am interested in history and eager to hear, even if it takes hours and days, even if uncle and mom get tired. I will not be fed up, and I'll listen a lot enthusiastically.

Fariba:

- I don't think it's that hard to hear the story. I want to hear it too. Even when I'm busy in the kitchen, I'll still pay attention to what you say.

Farhad:

- Well, now that dear Mobina loves her uncle's heart, I will listen too. I hope it is worth hearing.

Pirooz took a deep breath and said,

- My childhood life and my best companion, Ardeshir[1], are united. So, I have to say this. We belonged to the Vispoharan[2] or the great dynasties of Pars. Ardeshir's mother, Rudak, and my mother, Rudak's sister, were called Poopak. Their homeland was a place that was later named Ardeshirkhoreh, which means bright or the honor of Ardeshir. Considering their jobs, our fathers

---

[1] Ardashir I , also known as Ardashir the Unifier (180–242 AD), was the founder of the Sasanian Empire. Afterwards, Ardashir called himself "shahanshah" and began conquering the land that he called Iran. (Wikipedia)

[2] Waspohran or distinguished family is called the heads or generally people of big families in the Sassanid era. (Wikipedia)

lived in Istakhar, the center of the Pars government in those days, and we were born somewhere around Istakhr. From the very beginning of our childhood days, we were so attached that even at night, we used to sleep in the same bed. We were both interested in books and training in fighting techniques. The only difference between us was that he was more interested in fighting, like his father, Babak. And like my father, Nerseh, I was more interested in books. In those days, it was customary to separate boys from their families and send them to war training. When we were seven years old, we were sent to Argbod or Darabgerd fortress, one of the five great cities of Pars at that time and considered the military city of Pars."

Mobina:

- So, you are saying that Darabgerd[1] was circular before Ardeshirkhoreh? Everyone says that Ardeshirkhoreh is the first circular city in the world!

Pirooz:

- Ardeshirkhoreh is the first city that Ardeshir built before the rebellion against his father-in-law, the fifth Ordvan[2], since 211 A.D. when his brother Shapur died, and Ardeshir became the Gochahr or local king of Pars in Istakhr until 220 A.D. I experienced torture for nine years to reach my old

---

1 Darabgerd was the name of one of the five states of Pars in ancient Iran. It is also called Daragerd or Darabjerd. (Wikipedia)

2 **Artabanus IV**, also known as **Ardavan IV** incorrectly known in older scholarship as **Artabanus V**, was the last ruler of the Parthian Empire from c. 213 to 224. He was the younger son of <u>Vologases V</u>, who died in 208. (Wikipedia)

longing during my childhood. After finishing the construction of the city, Ardeshir, the government transferred the center of Pars to Ardashirkhoreh.

Mobina:

- So Darabgerd is the first circular city in the world?

Pirooz:

- Darabgerd is not the first circular city either. The initial base of this city was created in the form of military barracks and a small city during the time of Dariush the Great[1], the Achaemenid king who ruled 500 years before Christ, during the Parthian period, which began in 247 AD to 224 BD. It was expanded by the addition of new buildings that were mostly used for military purposes. It was built in the form of a large and prosperous city based on the military camps of the Assyrian government, which was formed in Miyanroodan.

Mobina:

- Miyanroodan?

Pirooz:

- Tazians called it Mesopotamia, a place between the Tigris and Euphrates rivers.

---

1 Darius I commonly known as Darius the Great, was a Persian ruler who served as the third King of Kings of the Achaemenid Empire, reigning from 522 BCE until his death in 486 BCE. (Wikipedia)

Mobina:

- So, the first circular city in the world was somewhere between these two rivers?

Pirooz:

- Maybe such a city was built before, but I have not read that anywhere.

Mobina:

- Did you say that Ardeshir's father was Babak? So why Sassanid?

Pirooz:

- Sasan was from Istakhr and was originally the guardian of the Anahid fire temple in the city. He married the daughter of Gochahr of Pars, named Ram Behesht, who was from the Bazarangi dynasty, and Babak was the result of this marriage.

Mobina:

- So, the name of Ardeshir's grandfather was Sasan?

Pirooz:

- Yes.

Mobina:

- Well, what happened after you went to the Darabgerd fortress at the age of seven?

Pirooz:

- We tried to seek knowledge in that place until we were young and mature. After the death of the commander,

Ardeshir became the commander of the Darabgerd fortress. At this time, Ardeshir built a magnificent palace next to a beautiful spring in his native land until his father, Babak, asked him to recognize the kingship of his eldest son, Shapoor, in Istakhr during the reign of the Parthian fourth Balash. But the emperor rejected this request, and as a result of this, Babak rebelled in 205 A.D., and Shapoor reigned in Istakhar. Later he and his father died, and Ardeshir, as I said before, went to Istakhr in 211 A.D., took his brother's place, and became Gochahr, the local king of Pars. From the beginning of his reign, the Parthian king, who later Ardeshir chose his daughter as his wife, that is, the fifth Ardavan, was against this government. After a long negotiation, the parties saw no option but to start the battle. Ardeshir Babakan brought his army to Khuzestan in the spring of 224 A.D. and settled in the strategic points of the Hormuzdagan plain. His location made him control the water resources of this plain. On the other hand, Ardavan, from the capital city of the Parthians, the city of Tisphoon, had gone to Hormuzdgan, but he was only able to settle in the less important places of the plain and had few water sources. On April 24, 224 A.D., the battle between the two armies began, and on the same day, the battle ended with the killing of the Ardavan. After that, on April 28, 224 A.D., Ardeshir was crowned emperor of Iran and called himself Artakhshatra or the holy Shahriyar and his land was called Iranshahr. Ardeshir, after the coronation, gave many rewards to his companions. In the meantime, I, the one who was deemed as his childhood friend, in a twosome party in the hidden library in Ardeshirkhoreh, asked him to let me spend my life studying and researching in that library, and Ardeshir accepted my desire and gave me a lot of wealth so that I can fulfill this wish on my own.

Farhad:

- So instead of premiership and government, you only wanted a library?

Pirooz:

- Yes, that's right. For many years, I was engaged in building a hidden library in the height of the Ardashirkhoreh region and doing research. I reported the results of my research with great enthusiasm during the Mehregan festival every year to my intimate friend and king, Ardeshir, in the twosome party, until one day in my old age, even though my body was trembling, I made a potion and drank it. After drinking, the trembling disappeared at first, which enchanted my body, and then the wrinkles on my body faded and disappeared. My hair turned into black color in a short time. I was shocked a little, and I was spinning headlong and enjoyed it because of the new power that came into my body. Suddenly, a prickle that had been passed through my hand for a very short moment quickly disappeared; when I looked at my hand, I saw a deep wound that was getting smaller moment by moment and disappeared after a moment. At first, I was scared, but after a while, when I cut my hand again, it quickly disappeared. I realized that I had reached a great achievement, and I had drunk the cup of life like a Pashootan. I went happily to Ardashirkhoreh and danced in the city. I thought of going to Tisphoon to give an early report to my friend, only to meet the news of the Ardeshir's death by the town criers. It ended my happy days.

Fariba:

- So, the news of your friend's death was heard on the same day?

Pirooz:

- I have seen a lot of bitterness in this precious life, but without a doubt, the most bitter event among them is related to February 242 A.D., when half of my life was rested in the soil that later became known as Naqshe Rostam[1]. Still, at the time of desolation, I feel the smell of that soil. I wish my knowledge had taken me to the place where I had gained the power to return Ardeshir to the earth. (He sighed and remained silent.)

A few moments later, Mobina asked,

- What did you do after Ardeshir's death?

---

1 Naqsh-e Rostam is an ancient archeological site and necropolis located about 12 km northwest of Persepolis, in Fars Province, Iran. A collection of ancient Iranian rock reliefs are cut into the face of the mountain and the mountain contains the final resting place of four Achaemenid kings, notably king Darius the Great and his son, Xerxes. (Wikipedia)

Pirooz:

- I secluded myself in my hidden library and mourned, but there was no choice but to start life again. I went to Bistoon as I was restless, maybe I could feel the relaxation sense by associating with his son, but my appearance was so young that they didn't see a sign of Pirooz in it. After insisting on meeting with Ardeshir's son, he said, *"We tried hard to find Pirooz, and in the end, we have received the news that Pirooz, like identical twins, after his soul mate's death, has moved from the tight wheel of life to be with his old friend Artakhshatra like the other days. The fact was that staying in Tisphoon was meaningless and boring when I saw the unkindness of people around Ardeshir."* Inevitably, I returned to Ardeshirkhoreh and started to research and study to a great extent again to achieve my big dream.

Mobina:

- Wasn't your greatest wish reaching eternal life?

Pirooz:

- No, it was my long-standing wish to reach the needless potion of human beings, which I still have not reached.

Mobina:

- The needless potion of human beings? So what?

Pirooz:

- To end all wars because I hate everything about war.

Fariba:

- That is interesting, but what does it have to do with war?

Pirooz:

- The reason for war is need: **women, land, power, wealth,** and thousands of other needs have become a bane of human life.

Farhad:

- Don't praise yourself so much. Tell me, what have you been doing all these years?

Pirooz:

- Many kings came and went, from the Sassanians to the Arabs and, recently, the Mongols. I saw many crimes. I lived secretly for over a thousand years and tried to find the potion. Now and then, I entered the city. Sometimes, I looked like a potion, and sometimes I was like a traveler. I had so many Sassanid treasures that I had no problem getting food and sex for thousands of years. But the desire of finding a solution to build a city for people devoid of evil was still burning inside me. I didn't share my secret with anyone and kept trying. The city, like its rulers and residents, would undergo many changes, and it would affect me. I had to learn an updated religion and language. The name of the city was changed from Ardeshirkhoreh to Gour and, recently, Jour. There has been some time when I presented myself as a traveler who is also a storyteller to the new inhabitants of my motherland, now known as Gour. Soon, the word of my sweet stories spread by word of mouth in the city, and many interested people, from children to teenagers and adults, men to women, all gathered around me and listened to my stories. The government of the time was watching my movements, and they concluded that people were more obedient and less violent because of my stories. For this reason, they had no issue with me. There was a great attraction to me from the women because of my stories, and the elders made me marry a woman to reduce this. After my pleading that I was a traveler and couldn't be married fell on deaf ears, I consented to a temporary marriage with a young widow named Ziba. In the morning, I went out of the city to find medicinal plants, and in my hidden library, I carried out experiments, research and study. In the evenings, I told stories and sometimes prescribed herbal medicine to patients. I became known as a skilled doctor. So, besides telling stories, I practiced medicine and was engaged in married life.

Fariba:

- Did you have any experience in the field of medicine?

Pirooz:

- From the knowledge I had gathered from reading, I was able to prescribe herbal medicines, but I did not have any desire for this. Experience taught me that if

I continued, I would be forced to live a life of a doctor. For this reason, I could not wait to be hidden again.

Farhad:

- He has started praising himself again. What happened next?

Pirooz:

- One morning, I succeeded in making a potion and took some of it to test it on someone. I returned to the city happily because I was busy telling stories of this to everyone. Messengers from the ruler of the city summoned me to the palace for medical treatment. As I had no intention of attending to the palace, I respectfully made an excuse and promised to go to kiss the ruler's hand tomorrow. After the messengers left, some fearless youths prevented me from leaving and spoke about the hard-heartedness of the Mongol rulers. When the night spread its black shadow on the wheel of the city, despite my strong attachment, I hugged my wife and started a conversation about separation and leaving. Among the romantic moments of tears and heartbreak, I suddenly remembered the potion I had completely forgotten. A thought crossed my mind, and I decided to test it on Ziba. I dropped a few drops into Ziba's mouth. Moments later, Ziba's eyes closed, and she slowly fell to the ground. Suddenly, she turned into a red light and disappeared.

Mobina:

- So, she disappeared so easily, and you didn't care?

Pirooz:

- It wasn't easy. I was wandering in a burning hell. For a few moments, I looked at the place where Ziba had been and cried. After a while, I wiped my tears and decided to leave the city and hide in my library for many years. I took my personal belongings and was going to leave, but I was forced to stop because of the strong attachment I had for the city, along with the torment that was embedded inside me. After confronting lots of difficulties, a thought crossed my mind. I had eternal life and leaped into the dark. I hung the small potion bottle around my neck, put drops of the potion in my mouth, closed the lid of the bottle tightly, and after a few moments, like Ziba, my eyes were closed.

Fariba:

- It means that you disappeared too?

Mobina:

- Well, where did you go?

Pirooz:

- When my eyes opened, I got up and found myself in an unfamiliar land. My surroundings were full of the same bushes, and I did not see any sign of insects or animals. I noticed footprints left on the ground and realized that it was probably Ziba's. I followed the footprints slowly and carefully, and after an hour, I heard sounds. I went towards the sound. I recognized Ziba's voice; it was like she was talking to someone else. At first, I wanted to shout Ziba's name, but I decided to continue silently so that if there was any danger, I could save Ziba with my martial techniques. I walked behind a bush to see Ziba, but I did not see anyone. I repeated this several times, but it was useless. Then I noticed something hard to believe; I rubbed my eyes and slapped myself. No, I wasn't dreaming. Ziba was talking to a tree. The tree noticed me and shouted, *"Oh, Ir, help me. Who is he?"* Ziba looked back with fear, then laughed after seeing me and said, *"Don't worry, he is my husband, Pirooz. Pirooz, come and see how interesting it is. I have found a tree that speaks. It is very sweet-spoken, like yourself."* I looked at my surroundings and approached her hesitantly. Then I walked around the tree several times in surprise. The tree laughed and asked, *"What happened? What are you looking for? I mean, have you never seen a tree?"* I scratched my head a little and said, *"Why? I know many trees well, but none of them speaks."* The tree laughed again and said, *"Here, the shrubs are dumb, but we trees talk to each other."* I asked, *"Are there other trees? I only saw shrubs."* The tree said, *"Here, the only trees are my wife and me. A little further in the left half, there is a Souch planet. It should be night and rainy there. I can see it from here, but you can't."* I asked surprisingly, *"Souch planet?"*

Farhad:

-       We just reached the Souch planet.

Pirooz:

- Have you gone to Souch too?

Mobina:

- No. Continue, and I will tell you later.

Pirooz:

- I asked surprisingly, *"The Souch planet?"* The tree said, *"Don't you know Souch?"* It laughed and continued. *"Souch planet, in the Ir system of Ann galaxy."* I said, *"If I am right, the name of your star should be Ir, and you worship it."* The tree said, *"You are so smart."* It laughed and continued. *"How did you know"*? I said, *"Well, as soon as you saw me, you said, 'Oh Ir, help me."* Ziba asked me worriedly, *"Pirooz, what did you give me that brought me here? Where are we? What does this tree say? How did you come here? Do we have a way back or not? What will happen to our family and friends?"* I said, *"My dear Ziba, wait a little, and I will explain to you. Both of us came with the help of the same potion, and we will likely return by it."* Ziba asked, *"Let me see. Where did you get this potion from? Who did you get it from?"* I said, *"I didn't get it from anyone. I made it myself."* Ziba asked, *"Does that mean my husband is a witch?"* I said, *"What do you mean by a witch?"* Ziba asked, *"If this is not magic, so what?"* I said, *"How many times should I say 'wait a little'? I will explain to you, but on the condition that you promise me to listen to my words until the end. Then be sure that you will get the answer to all your questions."*

Ziba said, "*I will try to be quiet.*" Then I told Ziba everything I told you about my childhood.

Farhad:

- You mean, you talked so much your wife listened silently? Is that possible?

Pirooz:

- Ziba interrupted my conversations 100 times and flirted in different ways while I told her my life story for hours when we sat beside the tree.

Fariba:

- Did Ziba accept your words?

Pirooz:

- No. At the beginning of her words, she asked, "*Do you expect me to believe that you are thousands of years old now? Does that mean I have eternal life now?*"

Farhad:

- She was right; these words are unbelievable.

Pirooz:

- After thinking for a short time, I took a piece of sharp stone and quickly cut Ziba's hand. Ziba said, "*what are you doing, stupid man?*" I said, "*We will both figure it out now.*" Ziba asked, "*What are you talking about?*" I said, "*Look at the wound on your hand.*" Ziba looked at the wound on her hand and saw it healing quickly. After a while, her hand was just like it was before the injury. Even the faint-colored wrinkles on her hand were gone, and her hands were similar to a youth's. I said, *"This means that you will always be young like me."* Ziba, who was so happy, said, *"Oh my God! Is it possible? Does that mean I'm not dreaming? Does that mean there is no more sign of wrinkles and aging?"* I pointed to myself and said, *"You can see me who experienced this years ago."* After a while, Ziba and I explored this new planet. We saw nothing but shrubs, two caves, and two Sishma trees. The most interesting thing was that we did not feel thirsty or hungry or need to go to the toilet. We did not get tired. It was like we had forgotten to sleep. There was not even a simple yawn.

Farhad:

-    He means no need to sleep.

Pirooz:

-    Yes. As I was saying, we were looking for shadows in the earth and hiding from the heat of the sun. But now, we have an infinite tendency towards the light. The languor of death faded away from our bodies by spreading a little shadow. We stayed with Ir's light, and the Souch planet had turned under our feet. It was night behind us and a soft rain that we could not see because it was in the dark, and we were running away from it. We had a warm conversation with both trees, which we called Sishma, and we found out that the name of the shrubs was Savich. Right in the middle of the planet, the shadows were shorter, and our movement toward the light was faster. Right in the middle, there were Sishma trees along each other, and two caves could be seen at the same distance. Although I wanted to search inside the caves, I was running away from its shadow, and I could not tolerate the shadow for a long time. Inevitably, I came out of it very early and got stronger again by reaching the light. As we went up or down from the middle beltway of the planet, the length of the trees' shadows got longer, and we moved slower when we followed the light. For a long time, the main option of our movement was the middle beltway, sitting beside the Sishma tree and telling stories to Ziba. As more time passed, the attractions of the planet became weaker, and Ziba's nag became more to the point where a verbal debate took place between Ziba and me. Ziba got angry and moved away from me. After a while, loneliness caused Ziba to stay with me and ask me gradually to return to the earth together, and I accepted.

Mobina:

- Does that mean you are tired?

Fariba:

- They were right. Is it possible to survive days and nights without a companion?

Farhad:

- Does that mean there were no animals?

Pirooz:

- Nothing, nothing. There was not even a fly.

Farhad:

- The absence of flies is a blessing, but no place is attractive without animal meat. How can you ignore broth? You weren't even hungry. That is not pleasant at all.

Mobina laughed and said,

- Uncle, you focus on meat all the time.

Fariba:

- By the way, I have made Abgousht[1] according to my dear Farhad's taste. It will be ready in an hour.

Mobina:

- Mom, you are only caring about your brother all the time.

Farhad:

- Jealousy. Don't worry; she will cook chicken rice for you tomorrow too.

Fariba:

- Now, as we have time, let our guest continue his story.

Farhad:

- I agree; it is worth listening to.

---

[1] Abgousht is a very traditional Persian food that made with lamb meat. (translator)

Mobina:

- Uncle Pirooz, what happened next?

Pirooz:

To say good bye, we decided to go towards the Sishma trees, which were my only friends during my stay. But before I left, I said goodbye to the first tree and then went towards the other tree, the same tree we saw for the first time after entering Souch. As soon as he saw us, he said, *"Do you intend to leave so soon?"* I said, "How did you know?" The tree replied, *"My wife said you intend to leave this planet. Why do you want to leave now?"* I said, *"To be honest, we are maddened by all these events. Ziba also misses her relatives and friends."* The tree said, *"There is a reason you are here. You have not discovered the biggest secret of this planet."* Ziba asked, *"Secret? Whatever we looked for, we did not find except for two talking trees."* The tree replied, *"The biggest secret of the Souch planet is inside it."* I said, *"We did not see a way to get inside the planet."* The tree said, *"At the end of every cave, there is a way into the planet. The Souch planet is as big as thousands of planets like Earth. As you enter it, you begin a Journey, a Journey that takes thousands of years."* Ziba said, *"The earth is full of domestic animals with delicious meats, colorful fruits, jewels and thousands of other things. We don't even eat here. Apart from that, we only saw similar shrubs and you two strange trees. If you were not here, this planet would have been more unbearable."* I said, *"Only God knows how much I have missed my library."* The tree said, *"The most interesting part of the Journey is that you will have whatever you want.*" I said, "*How?*" The tree said, "*Just ask. It will be ready in the blink of an eye.*" Ziba asked, "*Does that mean if I ask for gold pendants or diamond rings or pearl necklaces, I will have them?*" I said, "*I have these things.*" Ziba asked sadly, "*You don't have two pennies.*" I said, "*I have great treasures that belonged to Ardeshir in my hidden library.*" Ziba asked, "*Does that mean you had these things and deprived me of them?*" I said, "*If I did, it would have been to avoid curiosity and trouble. The least punishment for us would have been a dungeon and interrogations by the ruler.*" The tree said, "*There is no ruler in this Journey, and whatever you want, you will receive a thousand times more.*" I said, "*It is not possible. According to my calculations, the longest walk on the surface of planet will last 730 days but inside is Thousands of years? No, this is not possible.*" The tree said, "*How are you talking to me now I mean talking to the tree? Was it possible before you came?*" I said, "*We can't go toward the shadows on this planet, let alone the end of the cave.*" The tree said, "*I have the solution for this problem.*" Ziba asked, "*Really? I mean, can we go toward the shadows or sleep a little? I even miss sleeping on the earth.*" The tree said, "*Of course you can.*" I asked Ziba, "*My dear Ziba, should we start the Journey or return?*" Ziba said, "*I think there is no greater pleasure than hugging my mother and meeting friends and acquaintances. It is better to go back and bring everyone with us after ending our homesickness than start this Journey.*" I said, "*Yes, I can. It's not a bad idea. We will do that.*" The tree said, "*Now that you are going, I wish you a good Journey."* I said, *"I think I can do this."* Ziba said, *"I will accompany you to satisfy you as a woman."* I said to Sishma tree, *"We accept your condition. We will leave and return early, so see you soon."* Then I opened the lid of the bottle and dropped a few drops in Ziba's mouth. After a few moments, Ziba's eyes closed, then she fell on the ground slowly, turned into green light, and disappeared. I also drank drops, and my eyes were closed like Ziba's.

Mobina:
- Well, what happened next?

Pirooz looking upset about something and said,
- I am so sorry. I want a little time to leave the room and go to the gent as I have not voided for years.

Fariba looked at Farhad and asked,
- Gent? Voiding? What does he say.

Farhad:
- I didn't understand either, P300… no, who are you? Aha, Pirooz, we don't understand where you want to go.

Pirooz:
- How can I say it? Sneaky.

After a little silence, Pirooz noticed they did not understand what he meant. He got up, went towards Farhad, and whispered something in his ear. Farhad got up smiling, took his hand and led him to the restroom, opened the door and turned on the switch then returned.

When Pirooz heard the sound of the air conditioner, he became a little scared. He looked at it shockingly. He wanted to say something. He pressed the switch hesitantly, and the light and ventilation went off. Then excitedly, he repeated it many times.

Farhad:

- Don't do it. It will break down. It is not a toy. Why do you do that?

Pirooz:

- It is a great achievement. How does it work?

Fariba:

- God bless Edison.

Pirooz:

- Who is Edison?

Mobina:

- Inventor of the lamp.

Farhad:

- Turn on the light and go inside so you don't create problems for yourself.

Pirooz turned on the switch, went into the restroom and closed the door. After a while, Farhad, who seemed worried about Pirooz staying in the restroom for a long time, got up and went to the restroom. He knocked on the door and asked:

- Are you okay?

Pirooz:

- Yes.

Farhad:

- What are you doing? Do you have a problem? Are you constipated?

Pirooz:

- No, I was done a long time ago.

Farhad:

- Did you fall asleep?

Pirooz:

- No, I am studying the interesting phenomena of this strange place.

Farhad:

- Can I open the door?

Pirooz:

- Open it.

Farhad opened the door and saw Pirooz standing in front of the sink, constantly opening and closing the faucet to heat and cool it.

Pirooz:

- How is it possible that there is both cold drain water and hot drain water, easily mixed and sunk into a polished stone hole?

Farhad:

- What are you saying? What is drain?

Pirooz:

- Aqueduct.

Farhad:

- This is not aqueduct water. It is piped water. Do you know what a pipe is?

Pirooz:

- Yes, I have applied a new type of thin clay pipes in the palace.

Farhad:

- Move away from the faucet. It will break.

Then he took Pirooz's hand and turned him away, closed the door, turned off the switch and led him to sit down.

Mobina:

- (To Pirooz) I heard you say something about clay pipes. What were they?

Pirooz:

- Yes, when Ardeshir was building a magnificent palace on top of the Padena mountain, they dug numerous reservoirs in the mountain and connected them with thin clay pipes. This way, the water came from the river to the top of the mountain.

Mobina:

- You mean that the water would automatically rise from the riverbed to the Dokhtar Castle?

Pirooz:

- There are hot and cold rivers around you, and you have applied clay pipes to bring water here?

Mobina laughed and said,

- No. You are supposed to tell all the stories of your life, and then I will show you a way to answer your questions.

Fariba:

- My daughter is right. Finish the story of your life.

Pirooz:

- Honestly, I am so tired. I haven't slept or eaten anything for years.

While getting up, Fariba said,

- I'm sorry, I forgot. Mobina! come here and help us to prepare a dinner table.

A few moments later, the dinner table was set, and Farhad's favorate food, Abgousht, was eaten with great pleasure. Moments later, Pirooz's sat on the sofa and fell deep asleep. Farhad made his bed right there beside the sofa with the help of Fariba and Mobina. While mother and daughter were going

to their bedroom, Farhad called Pirooz slowly. He guided him
to the bed and said,

- I will sleep right here beside you. Call me if you need
  anything.

After a while, both of them fell asleep.

*****

Farhad shook Pirooz, whose face was wet with sweat and was
moaning. Pirooz woke, sat in bed, and looked around curiously.

Farhad:

- You were moaning. You didn't allow me to sleep.
  What were you dreaming about?

Pirooz:

- Ziba had stood at the opening of the cave. Strange
  roots were sticking out of the soil, and it had held her
  hands and feet hardly. As soon as she saw me, she
  screamed and asked for help. I ran towards her
  quickly. Suddenly, the soil opened, and I fell into a
  big hole, in which lots of big and small roots were
  seen. I grabbed a root to take myself outside, but
  suddenly, the root in my hand disintegrated after a
  sharp sound of laughter, and its particles scattered
  around. I fell again, grabbed the other root, and
  pulled myself up. Again, there was a sound of
  laughter, and this happened repeatedly. It was a
  weird and terrifying dream. I thought Ziba, Arash,
  and the fearless people of the Gour city called me for
  help.

Farhad:

- When you don't know where they are, how can you help them? We haven't heard the whole story of your life yet. Maybe we can solve the puzzle after. We can find a way.

Pirooz got up and went to the restroom. Later, Fariba and Mobina left the bedroom.

It didn't take long for the breakfast table to be set. After eating, it was cleaned up, and everyone sat.

Mobina:

- (eagerly) Uncle Pirooz, you didn't tell what happened next.

Pirooz:

- Which part of the story has been said?

Fariba:

- The part where you said goodbye to the Sishma trees and disappeared after eating the potion.

Pirooz:

- Yes. When I opened my eyes, I saw myself beside Ziba, who was looking around with surprise. Ziba said, *"What is going on in our house?"* I looked around and said, *"Our belongings are not here. The dust and cobwebs are the results of our absence. I think we have returned after a few months."* Ziba said, *"I feel so hungry, but there is nothing to eat."* I said, *"It is strange. I am so hungry that I cannot walk."* Ziba said, *"Let me get food from my mother. I know you don't like this situation, but there is no other way. This is the easiest way to solve this problem."* I said, *"Wait a little."* I went to the door of the room, took what I had hidden, and returned to Ziba. Ziba said, *"Wow, this is beautiful. Where did you get it?"* I said, *"I had hidden it in a corner just in case."* Ziba asked, *"Is it for me?"* I replied, *"It is mine but give it to your mother as a gift from the trip. Just be careful. Don't tell her about the strange happenings. Tell her we ran away at night for fear of going to the palace and we spent our time in different cities."* Ziba said, *"I will do so."* Then, she arranged her appearance a little and left the house. It didn't take long for her to return with a loaf of bread only. I asked, *"What happened? Has anything happened?"* She answered, *"I don't know. Except for my brother's wife, Mahvash, no one was in the house. After a little conversation, she gave me the only bread in the house and said, 'Don't worry, go and care for your husband. I will send your brother to talk with you soon."* I asked, *"Didn't she ask any questions?"* She answered, *"Yes, I said what you said, but the streets of the city had become so strange and deserted that I had many questions, but she didn't answer."* We shared the bread and ate it hungrily. After a while, we heard the sound of a knock on the door. A man and a woman were waiting outside the house to enter. Ziba went to the door and opened it. Ziba said, *"My sweet brother, Arash! Only God knows how much I missed you."* Then she turned toward Mahvash and continued. *"Mahvash, welcome. Where are the others?"* Arash said, *"Be patient. Let me catch my breath. I would tell you everything."* I joined them, hugged Arash, and after a short greeting, I invited them to come inside. I said, *"We have just arrived, and there is nothing in the house but this ragged mat. Do you have any news about our belongings?"* Arash said, *"About a month after your disappearance and your memorial, we moved your belongings to your father's house."* Ziba asked, *"Memorial ceremony?"* Arash answered, *"Yes. In the city, it was rumored that you were killed by the Mongol rulers. The news of this event spread from the city of Gour to our own Kooshk to Istakhar and Darabgerd and even the Siraf port. It spread and brought the freedom fighters together. An uprising took place under the pretext of your bloodlust, eventually leading to the city's liberation from the nefarious Mongols."* I asked, *"Uprising? Our bloodlust?"* Arash replied, *"Yes. Let me know, where have you been during this one year that you haven't heard about the news of the fearless uprising of Gour? How did you pass the siege of the Mongols and enter the city?"* I had already expected a question about how we escaped and had thought about the answer. *"Honestly, I had read in a book about the Sasanian era that an underground path was built in Ardeshirkhoreh, which we now call Gour, by order of Ardeshir. A few days before the arrival of the palace messengers, as I was looking for medicinal plants, I strangely found that path. Maybe it was God's will that we escape through that path when threatened by the palace. We moved away from this city as far as we could. Now, we came from the same path and did not notice the siege and the events you mentioned."*

Pirouz took a breath and continued:

- Arash smiled and said, *"Thank God for opening a way to save the defenders of the city so that they can keep their stability. The city has been under siege for more than two months now, and there is little food left. Many thanks to God for opening a way to save us from this famine."* Ziba asked, *"Does this mean that the people of the city have died because of the famine? Is this why the streets are quiet and without any passers-by?"* Mahvash answered, *"No, my dear sister. No one has died of hunger yet."* Ziba asked, *"So, where are the others? My parents, brothers, and sisters?"* Arash replied, *"Don't worry about them. I am sure they have been living in Kooshk. After the conquest of the city, it was decided that the elderly and children leave the city and settle in the surrounding settlements to be safe from the attacks of the Mongols. Some went to different cities in search of the fearless people who dreamed of freedom, and now with the arrival of the guests, nearly a thousand young couples watch the city. My only concern was finding a good way to provide food for my companions for the coming days."* I said, *"I know a better way."* Arash asked, *"Which way?"* I asked, "*Do you trust me?*" Arash replied, "*Yes. If we didn't love you more than our own eyes, there wouldn't have been an uprising because of you.*" I said, "*If that is the case, I will ask you to wait for three days, and then I will tell everyone. Now, I entrust Ziba to you and ask her to be silent until I return because I have to leave the city to do something. After three days, I will come with a liberating gift that you will not believe.*" Ziba said, "*I will come with you.*" I said, "*I am also very enthusiastic, but I need the shortest time to get results, and although your presence is encouraging, it would make us lose time. You have done the greatest service towards our goal by not talking for these three days and not changing the situation with your words.*" Ziba asked, "*You really won't leave me alone?*" In response, I said, "*If I had not been attached to and committed to you, I would have run away last year. Our goal is meaningless without each other's help. Didn't you promise to help me?*" Ziba answered, "*What you say is right. I will be your helper. I will wait for you.*" I said, "*During these three days, inform others of our return and tell them that I will come with great news and a liberating gift. Three loaves of bread are enough for me during these three days.*" Arash turned to Mahvash and said, "*Now get three loaves of bread from the food storage and bring them with you.*" Mahvash said, "*I will return as soon as possible.*" While Mahvash was on her way, I said to Arash, "*In three days, gather all the people in the city square in the middle of the night, I will join you to present the gift, and we will all suppress the sedition."* Arash said, *"It will happen."* After a few moments, Mahvash arrived with three loaves of bread. She gave them to me, and I went on my own to my hidden library. After three days of struggling and preparing what I wanted, I entered the main square of the city. I saw Arash talking to everyone around him. Arash: *"Thank God a thousand times for giving this city the honor of hosting the fearless people of the land of Pars, who will be a manifestation of the people's will to seek freedom and fight against the hard-hearted Mongols. Nearly two months have passed since the siege of the city, and we will keep our stability. I am proud of having such fearless companions."* Arash pointed towards me as he saw me, I made my way through the crowd and went towards him, and Arash continued. *"You are all aware of the return of our favorite doctor and his wife three days ago. Now, we have gathered to hear his words. I am just like you, ignorant and eager to know what the gift of liberation is; we have come to listen and suppress the revolt and make decisions together. But before that, I think it is better to inform you of the latest news from the messengers. According to different sours, at the beginning of the year 653 AH, Holako Khan, the brother of the great king of Mongol, after conquering most of the cities of Iran, planned to conduct a military campaign towards Egypt with a large number of warriors who were in the army to destroy the Gour and weaken our resistance. My goal is not to scare you, friends, because you, the fearless ones, have sacrificed your life, and you don't have any sense of fear. Now, here is Pirooz, the great doctor of the city."* After welcoming the people and urging them to be silent, I said, *"Peace be upon all of you, dear ones looking for freedom. It was a year ago that I ran away from this city with my wife, Ziba, but not in the way you can imagine. Before anything, let me say that I am neither a magician nor a chosen one who has come to guide you. I have read more books than anyone of you can imagine, for a thousand years, to achieve the great dream. I have started working on different combinations of different elements. You have heard various stories I told, many of which I have lived through and experienced. I have told you many of them from the books I have read. Remember what I said about Peshyotan[1], who drank a cup of milk from the hand of Zoroaster and reached eternal life? Or from a chosen one named Khezr, who has been living in anonymity among people for many years? I am none of them, but I made a potion and drank it. As I speak to you now, while I look forty years old, I have lived more than a thousand years."* An uproar arose from the crowd, and a person in the crowd said, *"Is it true what you are saying? Or is this one of your sweet stories?"* Another said, *"Is this the same as*

---

[1] Peshyotan is an <u>eschatological</u> figure of the medieval texts of <u>Zoroastrian</u> tradition, in particular in the apocalyptic <u>Zand-i Wahman yasn</u>. (Wikipedia)

your big wish?" I asked them to be silent and said, *"This was not my big wish, and it will not be. I will say more about it, but before that, I am with you people. Have you ever heard a lie from me? Or have I been greedy for the honor and wealth of others? Which one of you has been harmed by me?"* The uproar arose again in the crowd, and a person in the crowd said, *"What you say is right, but it is difficult to accept that you have lived for more than a thousand years now."* I said, *"It is not difficult. I will prove this to everyone, but before that, I say again, I am neither a magician nor the chosen one who has come to guide you. I have only read more books than anyone of you can think of for a thousand years. Now, one of you come near me and pierce a dagger in my heart."* The uproar arose again in the crowd, and a person in the crowd said, *"None of us is willing to do so."*

Pirouz looked at Farhad, Mobina and Fariba, who were only listening and not speaking. and continued:

-   I said again, *"It is not difficult. Take a good look now."* Then I pulled a dagger from the side of my shawl and cut my hand before their eyes. Some covered their eyes with their hands, and others stared in awe. I said, *"Be confident and watch closely."* A few moments later, the deep wound gradually healed, and my hand returned to its previous state. Again, a commotion arose in the crowd and chattering about magic and a chosen one. I asked them to be silent and said, *"I had imagined correctly.*

I say again. I am neither a magician nor a chosen one who has come to guide you. I've only read more books than anyone you can think of for a thousand years. This is the result of different combinations of multifarious elements I've tried. "A person among the crowd shouted, *"What a great achievement. Thank God, now we can build an immortal army like Cyrus, the great Achaemenid king, and take revenge against these bloodthirsty Mongols."* He laughed and continued, *"We will take back the great empire of Iran."* Again, there was a commotion in the crowd. I shouted, *"Let go of that. I will not agree with such a thing. I have a great hatred for all the war and bloodshed that is born out of need; the need for land, a woman, power, abundant wealth, and thousands of other needs that have become the bane of human life. If I wanted to do that, I would have done it alone a thousand years ago, and by now, I would be the supreme king of the earth."* There was a commotion in the crowd again, and a person from the crowd said slowly, *"We will take it from you forcibly."* I said, *"Don't be closed-minded. I have trained so hard to fight. None of you, alone or together, would be a worthy opponent. Just know that Artakhshatra and I, the great Sassanid Ardeshir, were one soul in two bodies. Now the sword is ineffective against me. I have more power. The other thing is that before you find my wife or me, we will be hidden, and you will never see a sign of us, as before, Ziba and I left."*

Pirouz continued:

- Someone among the crowd shouted bitterly, "*So why have you gathered us here? What do you want from us?*" I answered, "*I told you before that I had a big wish in my head. I wanted to create people with no needs and a city with nothing but beauty, free from any war and abomination, regardless of any ruler. Now, more than ever, I think I have achieved this long-standing dream in an unfamiliar land with the help of a friend named Sishma. Now, I'll ask Ziba to come up and shortly tell you about our Journey, the Souch land, and the words of our friend named Sishma.*" Ziba came up and said, "*Peace be upon you, kind people. Although we missed our family and friends, I now find myself among friends and a great family, which is a unique symbol. Let me tell you about the night that Pirooz came. He intended to escape from the city alone and go to his hidden library, which I found out after the trip. He goes there to hide for years. I recently found out that he had a lot of treasures and didn't tell me. Then he showed this jewelry.*" And everyone, especially the women, looked shockingly. I said, "*Leave these words for later. Now tell us about your Journey.*" Ziba continued. "*I had forgotten the place we were going had whatever we wanted. I told Pirooz I wanted to go alone. I don't know if he felt pity because of my crying or if he was interested in me that he didn't go; he himself said that he was interested in me. He poured drops of potion into my mouth, and my eyes closed. When I opened my eyes,*

I was alone in an unfamiliar land. To be honest, I was very scared at first, and tears were also coming out of my eyes. After a while, I saw that it was useless. Then I decided to look for someone or shelter, but there was nothing but bushes. Among them, I saw a tall tree, and I went toward it. Suddenly, someone said, Who are you? Where did you come from? I was very scared. I looked for the voice in the surroundings. As I was crying, I said I had come from the city of Gour. I was alone and defenseless. I was still looking for the voice in the surroundings when the voice said again, "What are you looking for?" The voice was from the side of the tree. Wiping my tears, I tried to see its branches; maybe my husband had sat there, but no one was there. I turned around the trunk of the tree; there was no one. I thought that I was dreaming because of loneliness. I said to myself, maybe someone is hidden behind the tree trunk. I went to the tree slowly and hit the tree with my hand several times. Suddenly, a branch came towards me and pushed me back slowly and said, "Are you crazy? Why are you hitting me? Did I hit you?" I asked surprisingly, "Do you expect me to believe that it is you"? Tree said, "Do you see anyone other than me?" I said, "No." He said, "So what are you saying? You didn't say how you came here?" I was telling him that Pirooz had arrived as well, and he was surprised to find that I was talking to a tree. I (Pirooz) pointed to Ziba and said, "My dear Ziba, "you are supposed to talk briefly. Time is short, but do not tell the story in detail." Ziba said, *"When we left at night, we didn't need to eat, drink, sleep, use the restroom, or even wash in that land. We just went around and had fun and enjoyed being together. Even our clothes were just like they were on the first day. We were only bothered by homesickness, and we decided to return and went to the two Sishma trees to say goodbye. The second tree said, 'you have not yet achieved the great secret of that land. There is a place as big as thousands of lands in that land, and whatever you want will be available to you in the shortest possible time. We decided to return and take our family, friends, and acquaintances with us and be happy together forever. Now all of you are my family, anyway. What about my parents?"* I replied, *"Let's specify this group's duty. We will focus on them later."* Again, there was uproar in the crowd, chattering about going and not going.

Pirouz took a glass of water from the table and drank some water. He had not felt thirsty for a long time, but now he felt how thirsty he was. And after drinking water, he continued:

- I urged them to be silent and said, *"Wait and suppress the murmurs. I will never ask you to be our companion forcefully. Now, according to what I heard about the great army of the Mongols coming in this direction, you have several options. First, escape from the city through a secret route, but be sure that the evil-doing Mongols will not stop until they catch and kill you. This is a lesson that I learned from them with time. Even if this condition doesn't happen again, the shame of running away until the moment of death is on your forehead.*" An uproar arose in the crowd, and there were discussions about running away or staying. A person in the crowd said, "*What is the other way?*" In response, I said, "*The second way is to provide food from the same hidden place and fight until you have the power to be killed proudly.*" Gradually, a few people started to talk, and then most people said, "*We will die with honor. We will not accept shame, and our name will be immortal.*" I raised my hands, asked them to be silent, and said, "*I have seen people like you. Your name will be remembered as a good symbol, but you will be forgotten much sooner than you think.*" A person in the crowd asked: "*So what should we do?*" I said, "*The other way is that, after a few days or a few weeks, I will prepare some potion so that you can hide from their eyes by drinking it. Then you attack the Mongol army and conquer them in battle.*" Again, there was a commotion in the crowd, and there were discussions about whether it would happen. A person in the crowd said, "*Is such a thing possible?*" I said, "*Be sure that it will happen, but there is a big problem.*" Someone in the crowd asked, "*What problem can be created?*" I said, "*The big problem is that you would be an invisible army forever, protecting the city. You will not be able to return to your previous form or even go to other places.*" The crowd was chattering, and someone said at the end, *"This means that we will become wandering spirits of Gour city. No, it is not a good idea at all."* Another asked, *"Is there another way?"* I said, *"The last way is that I will give you a potion so that we can travel with each other and enjoy life forever. Anytime you want, you can come back here by drinking the potion and continue your normal life, but your life will not be eternal anymore. Now, I will go with Ziba to the height of Bab-e-Hormoz, the same gate that opens towards the fire temple and the Qal'eh Dokhtar[1] at sunset. I am waiting for my fellow travelers. Ziba and I have decided to travel, with or without your presence. Now, shut your yapping and make your decision."* While the crowd was chattering, I took Ziba's hand. We came down from a height and went toward Bab-e-Hormoz. On the way, I asked Ziba to hide from the sight of the Mongols and be the only observer because then she didn't have eternal life. Then we went to the height of Bab-e-Hormoz, and I showed myself to the Mongol. Several arrows were thrown at me. I pulled out some arrows that pierced my body and threw the arrows toward them, which were covered in my blood and said, *"I will not die if you shoot at me for another thousand years. I will not fight with you either. I just ask you to listen to my words and transfer them to your commander."* One of the Mongols asked, *"Is such a thing possible?"* I said,

---

1 Qal'eh Dokhtar: (The Maiden Castle"), is a castle made by Ardashir I, in present-day Fars, Iran, in 209 AD. It is located on a mountain slope near the Firouzabad-Kavar road. (Wikipedia)

"I don't need to prove my words. I am not a magician, but take a look for yourself and listen to my words." then I cut my hand, and the Mongols saw its healing. Then I said, *"I am not interested in war and bloodshed. Otherwise, I would build an eternal army and take not only you but your generation from the earth. Now, I just want one thing, and I will leave the city to you tomorrow. I ask you to spend tonight in peace and just watch. We will not harm you."* At sunset, on the heights of Bab-e-Hormoz, right before the eyes of the Mongols, 729 young couples, along with a ten-year-old teenager who had stayed in the city from the beginning because of the other's insistence, put down their weapons one by one, drank drops of the potion, and turned into a red light and went to the sky. I gave the address of the hidden way that I had already marked to the few remaining. I asked them to run away as soon as possible, move away from the city of Gour, and not say anything about the events they saw because they would be called mad by the people. Then, Ziba and I drank drops of the potion and went to the Souch planet.

Mobina turned to Farhad and asked,

- Dear uncle, do you remember what I said about the sudden abandonment of Gour city from Wikipedia? Don't you think that's the reason?

While Farhad thought deeply, Pirooz asked Mobina,

- Who is Wikipedia?

Mobina,

- You will understand soon.

Farhad:

- It doesn't seem unlikely. Perhaps the Mongols who saw the lights that went to the sky and the people that disappeared would have been confused. They would have seen the city abandoned the next day and must have feared the unknown ones in the city. Their best solution was to go to Holako's army after looting everything left in the city and ruining some places, which included the gates and the city fence, to report to the great Khagan's brother.

Mobina:

- Yes, it is possible, but why haven't people returned to the city?

Fariba:

- Be sure that some of those who had escaped, spilled the beans and had said some things.

Farhad:

- That's right, that's it. Telling tales. People have never come to this city because of the fear of the unknown people who have settled in the city of Gour. The city is abandoned.

Fariba:

- (to Pirooz) Was the potion you drank different from others?

Pirooz:

- No, what do you mean?

Fariba:

- You have come alone, and others are not with you.

Farhad:

- (laughs) Dear Fariba, you talked about eating, so are you thinking about lunch?

Fariba:

- I also want to listen. We will eat hastily prepared food today. (Laughing) We will go eat out on to Farhad.

Farhad:

- The last thing I need now is to let my wife know that I have taken my sister to a restaurant and didn't take them.

Fariba:

- Well, tell them to come too.

Farhad:

- Definitely.

Pirooz:

- Restaurant?

Mobina:

- You will understand soon.

Pirooz:

- It's annoying. I have never been this ignorant in my life. It is a severe punishment.

Mobina:

- Don't you want to help your companions sooner?

Pirooz:

- Exactly, I do.

Mobina:

- So, tolerate a little. I think there must be another solution other than the potion. Continue your story. Maybe we will understand.

Pirooz:

- After I opened my eyes, I found myself in a circle of fearless people. Ziba, standing next to Mahvash, said, *"He came himself. Soon, everyone's assignment will be clear."* I said, *"Have they all arrived safely?"* Arash said, *"Yes, we all are here."* I asked, *"Is there any problem?"* Mahvash said, *"No, but a few people fainted recently."* I asked, *"Where are they? Show me."* After observing them, I asked that they be pulled from the shadow of the Savich bushes. A few people pulled them out quickly, and they regained consciousness after a while. Then I addressed them all and said, *"From now on, we are not interested in any shadows. Stay away from the shadows and stay with the light. We all live with light until Sishma tells us the solution. I want a little time to know which way is right for moving."* I looked around a bit and said, "*Come with me to go towards Sishma.*" I started walking, and others followed me. An hour later, we arrived at the tree. I turned to Sishma and said, "*This is another greeting that I promised. Peace be upon our good friend, Sishma. Now it's time for you to show us the way to reach the great secret of the Souch planet.*" The Sishma tree, who looked very happy, said, "*Only Ir knows how happy I am to meet you. My wife grumbled and blamed me for not protecting lovely companions Ziba and Pirooz. Now, it is time to tell her you returned happily. Don't hurry away. Let me and my wife be slaked by seeing you again for a few days and know the names of your companions.*" I said, "*Definitely, after knowing the great secret of the Souch planet and before leaving here, we will have a warm talk with you for many days. Now, there is no rush to start the Journey into the Souch planet, but it is better that you show us the way to reach the Souch planet's great secret so that my fellow travelers can relax and not return.*" Sishma said, "*Now that you are in a hurry, there is no choice; choose a little person among you to climb above me. I will take care of him and tell him what to do.*" The ten-year-old boy came forward and said, "*I am the youngest one among them.*" Sishma said, "*Congratulations to you. What is your name?*" The boy answered, "*Shapoor.*" Sishma said, "*I had heard the prince's word. What does Shapoor mean?*" I said, "*Shapoor is the same as Shahpoor, which means the son of the king or lord. It is also called*

Shahzadeh." Sishma asked Shapoor, "*You mean you are the son of a king?*" I said, "*No, it is only a name.*" Sishma asked, "*Is it fake? Isn't he a lord?*" I said, "*No, I said that it is only a name. Many have such names.*" Sishma pulled its branch down towards Shapoor and said, "*Little prince of great courage, take my branch and climb up.*" Shapoor took the branch and pulled himself up quickly. It didn't take long, with the help of Sishma, for him to get over the tree. He was picking up something that could not be seen clearly from below. Shapoor came down while his head carried something. Sishma said, "*Now, all of you should come close to Shapoor in an orderly fashion and take a seed and keep it carefully in front of yourself until I tell you what to do later.*" A few moments later, all of us were with seeds in our hands. We were watching Sishma and waiting for its words. Sishma said, "*Open the skin of the seed and take out the kernel. After that, I would say three things in a row. Then put them all together in your mouth and start chewing. It is a seed that is very sweet and enjoyable. It is only necessary that you all act together without hesitation. Otherwise, you will never achieve what you wanted.*" A few moments later, Sishma said, "*Are you all ready to go on a long and enjoyable Journey?*" They all agreed enthusiastically. Sishma said, "*Well done to all of you. You can see what a pleasant taste it has. Hey kid, what is your name? I remember, Shapoor.*" That was as far as I heard, and I saw myself here in these tacky clothes. I am now worried about my friends. Where are they, and what are they doing?

Mobina:

- So, the only information you know about Souch is this?

Pirooz:

- Yes, I said everything exactly.

Mobina:

- Ps and Zs? Had the high wall separated the Souch into two halves, right and left?

Pirooz:

- There is no wall in Souch. What are Ps and Zs?

Farhad:

- It is interesting. After drinking apple juice, he forgot all the things he had said before. If he drinks orange juice, he will not know Pirooz as well.

Mobina:

- Well done, my dear; that's it.

Farhad:

- What? Orange juice.

Mobina:

- No, amnesia.

Pirooz:

- Amnesia? But I didn't forget anything.

Fariba:

- Does he have Alzheimer's? He is young.

Pirooz:

- Alzheimer's?

Fariba:

- Amnesia disease?

Pirooz:

- I know the meaning of being psycho, but I don't see any signs of craziness in myself, and I don't need a bughouse.

Farhad:

- What is bughouse?

Pirooz:

- Somewhere outside the village, where such people are abandoned until their death time. I don't like this, and I am always trying to improve it. That's why it is not common in Gour city and nearby settlements, but I have heard about it from distant villages.

Mobina:

- But I didn't mean Alzheimer's.

Fariba:

- So, what are you saying?

Mobina:

- Uncle Pirooz said that he was here after chewing the kernel of the sweet seeds of Sishma.

Farhad:

- Well? What do you mean?

Mobina:

- Most probably, he forgot the past by eating it and has been in this condition for about 800 years.

Pirooz:

- It was a little before I came here. How is it possible? Does it mean that I ate it about 800 years ago?

Farhad:

- So how did he say all these events about the distant past?

Pirooz:

- I have only said a few words about my life because I was bored. I didn't say anything for nearly a thousand years of my life, and I remember every moment, from the succession of Ardeshir Babakan to the conquest of this land by the Mongols. If I want to retell the most important events, we would need years.

Mobina:

- Whatever I think, it cannot be anything other than what I said.

Fariba:

- Hoeny, whatever you say is right. So how does he know so much about the past?

Mobina:

- I don't know, maybe something caused it…Yes, that's it! Apple juice?

Farhad:

- Apple juice? What does it have to do with it?

Mobina:

- Do you remember what he said before you gave the apple juice to P300 forcefully?

Farhad:

- He said that *"If I eat it, I will be cursed by Ir"* or something like that. I still don't understand what it has to do with it.

Mobina:

- Did you notice that P300 used to be silent and put his hand on his forehead when he didn't know anything?

Fariba:

- I also noticed. I thought he was thinking, or his head was aching.

Mobina:

- No, Sishma's leaf was talking to him before taking the apple juice. If you have paid attention, the Sishma leaf or Sishma sees everything with P300's eyes. After eating, he does not put his hand on his forehead anymore.

Farhad:

- What are you saying? Do you watch fiction movies a lot, my dear?

Mobina:

- If I am not mistaken, all these events are related to Sishma.

Pirooz, who had sat quietly, listening carefully to their words and thinking, asked,

- What do you want to say, girl?

Mobina:

- Contrary to the image you have of Sishma, it deceived you.

Pirooz:

- What trick?

Mobina:

- The Souch planet has no big secret. It lied to keep you and Ziba in Souch.

Pirooz:

- Why?

Mobina:

- To get the heart of the other Sishma tree that you said was its wife.

Pirooz:

- But it wished us well for our journey and left us.

Mobina:

- This leaving was due to cupidity. Otherwise, it would have done the same with you and Ziba at that moment by eating the kernel of sweet seeds.

Farhad:

- Cupidity? Why cupidity?

Mobina:

- A bigger gift for its wife.

Fariba:

- A bigger gift?

Mobina:

- Yes. When Ziba mentioned returning with their family and friends, the fire of this greed fell into Sishma's life, and it made a bet to tell the great secret of the Souch planet.

Pirooz:

- If this was the case, it would have acted immediately after seeing us. But it said we should spend a few days in Souch so that we could get to know each other better.

Mobina:

- Yes, that's it. It wanted to know your name and deeds in these few days and know more about Earth by listening to your words, but as soon as it heard a word that referred to returning, it got to work.

Pirooz:

- Yes, it is possible. I told it that it would be better to show us the way to reach the great secret of the Souch planet so that my fellow travelers could relax and not return.

Mobina:

- That's it. After hearing this, fearing your return and its wife's grumblings, it quickly fulfilled its plan.

Fariba:

- What plan?

Mobina:

- Eating the sweet kernel of its seeds and then forgetting them.

Farhad:

- What will happen?

Mobina:

- It is clear. They all can stay there.

Pirooz:

- All the words that the young lady said have created a great doubt in my soul. How can I get rid of this doubt?

A few moments passed in silence, and then Mobina said,

- I got it, the Sishma leaf.

Farhad:

- Sishma leaf?

Mobina:

- Yes, it will clarify everything. We must find it as soon as possible. If I am not mistaken, a great danger threatens Pirooz.

Fariba:

- What danger?

Mobina:

- If Sishma has seen the events through Pirooz's eyes, it will look for ways to hide its bad deeds.

Fariba:

- From whom?

Mobina:

- From others who are in Souch.

Farhad:

- What can a tree do to be considered a threat?

Mobina:

- I don't know, maybe it will send P300 or someone else for forgetting him, and he will follow its mission.

After a while, the sound of the bell broke the silence. Mobina went towards the door phone, picked up the phone, and answered,

- Yes, please.

Caller:

- I am looking for P300. Tell him to come out.

Mobina:

- Sure, I would tell him now.

Farhad:

- Who is he?

Mobina hung up the phone and said,

- Someone in a soldier's uniform says he is looking for Pirooz, and I should tell him to come out.

Pirooz turned to Fariba and asked,

- How did Mobina talk with that voice?

Fariba:

- By door phone.

Pirooz:

- Door phone?

Farhad:

- Go to the door of the yard. They are looking for you. I will tell you after you come back.

Pirooz got up and went to the yard. A few moments later, Farhad's phone rang, and he answered,

- Yes, please...now.

He turned off the phone and ran to the yard. Hurriedly, Fariba and Mobina followed him, and a few moments later, Pirooz and Farhad dragged the soldier and brought him into the yard.

Fariba:

- What are you doing with the soldier? Do we have a little trouble?

Farhad:

- He is not a soldier.

Mobina:

- How did you know?

Farhad:

- Police just called me. Now, bring a rope, or anything.

Mobina went back inside.

*****

A few minutes later, the soldier was inside the house with his hands and mouth tied, and Farhad was talking on the phone. Pirooz looked at him shockingly.

Farhad turned off the phone, and Pirooz asked him,

- What is this? Who were you talking with?

Farhad:

- It is not good to be curious when another is on a cell phone.

Pirooz:

- cell phone?

Mobina:

- A new device that allows us to talk to or see each other from a distance.

Pirooz:

- How?

Mobina went toward the yard while making a video call with her uncle. She said,

- My dear uncle, answer me.

Farhad picked up the phone, went towards Pirooz, and said,
- In this way.

Mobina:

- Hello, Uncle Pirooz. It's Mobina. I was by your side now. Did you notice?

Then he hung up and went inside.

Pirooz stared at the phone with astonishment and, after a few moments of silence, said,

- My God, even Jamshid did not have this. How is it possible? Do you have any connection with royalty?

Mobina:

- Again, the same question. I said no, most people have cell phones.

Pirooz sat on the ground beside the wall and, after a few moments, continuously hit his head on the wall.

Farhad:

- Why do you act like that? Crazy?

Pirooz:

- How can I make up for nearly 800 years of unawareness? Woe to me. How? How? How can I compensate for such ignorance? I have to get to work right now. No. First, I have to emancipate my companions, but how?

Mobina:

- Don't worry, Uncle Pirooz. We will help you.

Fariba:

- My daughter is right. We will help you as much as we can. Do not stress yourself.

Mobina:

- Don't worry, you will save your friends, and I will show you a way to understand everything quickly. Get up. Now is not the time to despair. We must get to work.

Farhad:

- Yes; first of all, we must discover who this soldier is and where he comes from.

Pirooz:

- He is Arash, my brother-in-law.

Mobina:

- Did he say it himself?

Pirooz:

- No, he says that he is P320. As soon as I saw him, I got happy and hugged him and said, *"Hi, dear Arash."* But he answered me coldly and said, *"I am P320, and Sishma has sent me to save you from the curse of Ir."* Then he pulled my hand and took me forcibly. When Farhad came, we brought him here with each other's help.

Fariba:

- Why did you close its eyes and ears so tightly?

Mobina:

- So that Sishma cannot see or hear.

Farhad laughed, turned to Fariba, and said:
- Please give me a glass of apple juice. He will be Arash soon.

A few moments later, Fariba gave a glass of apple juice to Farhad, and he went towards P320. Mobina said suddenly,
- No, wait.

Farhad:

-   Why?

Mobina:

-   Arash cannot solve our problem. We need P320.

Fariba:

-   Why?

Mobina:

-   To find the Sishma leaf. P320 knows where it is, but Arash doesn't, or rather, Arash will forget about P320.

Fariba:

-   P320 does not cooperate with us. How are you going to convince him to do this?

Mobina took the apple juice from Farhad, drank it ceaselessly, and laughed, saying,

-   My amnesia should get better too. I don't know. We have to think about it.

Farhad turned to Fariba and said with smile,

-   My dear, I think I lost my train of thought too. No, I think my eyes have become purblind to a great extent. Where are you, my dear sister, I can not see you?

Fariba laughed and said,

-   Yes, now I will make carrot ice cream for everyone.

Pirooz:

- Can I see how you make the carrot juice through the device? What is ice cream?

Mobina:

- Let's go to see the kitchen appliances. Just look and get familiar with their names. You will know them all soon. Just be patient and don't be restless, okay?

Pirooz accepted, and they went to the kitchen.

*****

After a while, they sat on the sofa, drinking carrot ice cream.
Pirooz:

- Today, I am jealous of your people's condition. You are truly happy and prosperous and grateful to the incomparable God as you have all these new devices that produce pleasant taste.

Fariba:

- Contrary to what you imagine, the more people's facilities increase, the less they remember God and give thanks.

Pirooz:

- How is it possible?

Farhad:

- My dear, take it easy. I am not in the mood to participate in an education conversation. Tell me what to do with this P320.

Mobina:

- Let's give him a few drops of apple juice so he can know Pirooz.

Pirooz:

- No, he may remember all of Arash's memories by just a few drops or become insane. He is our only way to reach our goal, and testing him is costly.

Mobina:

- P320 likely has the black seed of Sishma with him. can you search inside his clothes?

Farhad:

- (smiling) Sure, Miss Marple.

He got up.

A few moments later, Farhad returned with something in his hand, seed-like hazelnuts, slightly smaller, with soft and black skin. Farhad took the seed toward Pirooz and asked,

- Is this what you wanted?

Pirooz took the seed and, after examining it, hid it in his clothes and said,

- Yes, that's it. I should examine it as soon as possible.

Mobina:

- I guessed correctly. We should become like Sishma.

Farhad:

- Do you want to become a tree?

Mobina:

- Uncle, don't play the fool. I am serious.

Then she started to explain.

*****

After the end of Mobina's dialogue, Farhad said,

- Wait a little. I will tell you, my opinion.

Then he went to the yard of the house. After some time, he returned and said,

- I also agree. So, when should we start?

Mobina turned to Farhad and said,

- My dear uncle, please come for a few minutes. I have something to do with you.

Then he went towards the yard, and Farhad followed her.

Farhad:

- My dear? What are you saying?

Mobina:

- Did you talk to the case agent?

Farhad:

- How did you know?

Mobina:

- The apple doesn't fall far from the tree. What did she say?

Farhad:

- She said we should make sure that both of them don't run away. If they do, we could end up in jail. They will come to take them away at night.

Mobina:

- Uncle, I have a question. Did you believe Pirooz?

Farhad:

- What can I say? Both yes and no.

Mobina:

- Answer from the bottom of your heart. My heart testifies to his truth and honesty.

Farhad:

- Me too nearly, so what?

Mobina:

- Uncle, just imagine, Pirooz was the most knowledgeable of his time, and now his knowledge is less than a child. I feel pity for him so much. I want to help him save his wife and others. Can you help me?

Farhad:

- Your words are looking for trouble. I cannot tolerate the detention center anymore.

Mobina:

- Don't worry.

Farhad:

- What do you want to say?

Mobina:

- Do you want to help or not?

Farhad:

- I said that if there is no problem, I will help.

Mobina:

- Don't worry.

Then she gave Farhad a piece of paper and started to explain.

*****

Pirooz get up P320 and said,

- P320, what are you doing here? Why are you being cooped up? Where did you get these clothes?

P320:

- You cooped me up yourself.

Pirooz:

- Me? It's so unlike P300 to do this to P320.

Farhad:

- What do I hear, P300 again? It is strange.

P300:

- What is strange?

Farhad:

- Weren't you Pirooz?

P300:

- Who is Pirooz? I am P300, the savior of the Souch planet. Don't you remember we came together to help me?

Farhad:

- What happened to him again?

Mobina:

- How many times did I tell you not to let him eat?

Fariba:

- Do you mean the black seed?

Mobina:

- Yes, that's what I am saying. When Pirooz said, "I *know this seed. I still remember its sweet and pleasant taste,*" and then he started to eat, how many times did I tell you not to let him eat?

Farhad:

- You are the witness; before I got to Pirooz, the damage was done.

Mobina:

- Because you delayed.

Farhad:

- Don't worry, my dear. I would give both apple juice so everything would be okay.

Mobina:

- Yes, Uncle, I would also like to know the story of Arash's life.

P300:

- Who is Arash?

Farhad:

- Don't you remember? You said that he was Arash.

P300:

- Why do you talk in vain? I have never said such a word.

Farhad:

- When you drink sips of apple juice, everything will be okay.

P300:

- But we Ps don't eat anything. If we do so, we will be cursed by Ir.

Farhad:

- If you don't do that, you will be cursed by me.

Fariba:

- Farhad, stop it. There was one person then, now there are two people, and you will not fight with them.

Farhad:

- I will. I will do it very well.

Fariba:

- Farhad! How late do you want to make trouble? Instead of showing these ridiculous fooleries, help P300's mission to be ended and leave here soon. Are you bored?

Farhad:

- Sure. Anyway, what Fariba says is right.

P300:

- I don't know what you are talking about. Anyway, we Ps don't eat anything; we live with the help of light and air.

P320:

- P300, are you really P300?

P300:

- So, you expected me to be P365? It's just like I've forgotten hours of my life. I'm so happy to see you. Have you come to help me? What is going on in Souch?

P320:

- From the moment you landed on the earth, we have been with you and heard Sishma's words until you were caught by the officers. We all put our chests on the ground according to what Sishma said and asked Ir loudly to help you. Sishma said you have eaten something and are cursed by Ir, and someone should volunteer as soon as possible and bring the life-saving medicine to help you.

P300:

- You didn't say where you got these tacky clothes.

P 320:

- Before the Journey, according to Sishma, I had to lay on my back on the ground and remain silent. It pulled down a branch and placed a leaf on my forehead as soon as I landed on the ground. I went to the house of the same man from whom you got the clothes and told him that, "As you are the trustee of my friend, I want a military uniform for filming," and he got it from a neighbor and brought it for me.

P300:

- Get up. We have to finish the mission as soon as possible.

P300 put a hand on his forehead and was silent for a moment. Then he continued,

- Oh, Ir help me, why doesn't Sishma talk to me? This is a great torment.

P320:

- Don't worry, he is talking to me.

P300:

- What should we do now?

P320:

-   We have to look for the stone.

P300 turned to Farhad and said,

-   Bring the stone so we can go.

Farhad:

-   The stone is not here. The officers took it with them.

P300:

-   Woe to me. What should we do now?

P320:

-   Don't worry, I know.

P300:

-   You don't know, and this is not a good thing. We should find a solution so I can know if we need to be separated from each other.

Mobina:

-   There is no need to think. Put the Sishma leaf on your forehead again because it talked to you before.

P300:

-   Well done. (Then he put his hand on his forehead and was silent for a moment. He moaned and continued). Oh, Ir, help me, what happened to me? Why don't I remember many things?

Mobina:

-   It is because of the black seed you ate.

P300:

- But I haven't eaten anything. We Ps do not eat anything.

Farhad:

- The same medicine that P320 said.

Fariba:

- You ate the same seed, don't you remember?

P300:

- No.

P320:

- I told you there is no need to be worried. Let us finish your mission, and then we will go toward the Sishma leaf and return to Souch by eating a red seed.

P300:

- But I want to hear Sishma's words as soon as possible. I miss its words.

Farhad turned to P320 and said,

- Don't you want P300 to help you?

Mobina:

- He definitely wants to be the savior of Souch planet on his own.

Fariba:

- He would have done something so that P300 could also help. Maybe he is jealous.

P320 put his hand on his forehead and was silent for a moment, and then he said,

- We do not understand jealousy. We will lose a lot of time going to return to the leaf.

Farhad:
- There is no need to be worried. We will go by car. It won't even take an hour.

P300:
- Car?

Mobina:
- It is the new chariot. It is much faster and more comfortable. It also has another advantage, which is that you get to know about the car more after returning. You'll have something new to say to others.

P300:
- Where would we get it?

Mobina:
- Uncle Farhad has it.

P320 put a hand on his forehead and was silent for a moment. Then, he said,
- If time would not be wasted, there is no problem.

Farhad:
- So, get ready to go.

Mobina:
- My uncle will come too.

Farhad:
- It is not necessary.

Fariba:
- My brother, it's been a long time since you took us outside. We are also coming to change our mood. We will buy some food for lunch from the restaurant.

Farhad:
- You know better. Arash and I always have recreational equipment in the car trunk. You can see that P320 is in a hurry.

Mobina got up happily, went to the bedroom, and said,
- We will come now.

Fariba also went behind him.

A few moments later, as Mobina and her mother were dressed to leave the bedroom, there was something in Mobina's hand.

Farhad:
- I see you have a pack in your hand, as usual.

Mobina:
- Uncle! Do not bother me.

*****

P300 eyed the car a little and said,

- So where are the horses of this chariot?

Farhad put his hand on the hood of the car and said,

- There are about 10 or 20 horses eating hay inside this area.

P300:

- But a horse cannot fit here.

Mobina:

- Uncle is joking. This chariot works with engine power.

P300:

- Engine?

Farhad:

- It contains the ring, piston, crank, cylinder, and thousands of other parts. If you are going to ask questions when you see something new and want to know how it works, we will not concentrate on anything else.

Fariba:

- In my opinion, P300 should be patient so that he can get to know everything at the right time.

Mobina:

- P300, first, let's solve the problem of finding Sishma leaf. Then you will understand everything.

They all got in the car. Farhad started the car and pressed the gas pedal a little after turning on the ignition.

P320, who looked a little scared, asked,
- What is this sound? What happened?

Farhad:
- The horses, as I said. They all neigh together.

P320 put a hand on his forehead and said,
- But this is not a horse's neigh.

Farhad:
- No.

Mobina:
- Anyway, I suggest we take a vow of silence until we reach our destination.

P320:
- Who is a vow of silence? Who should we get?

Farhad, Fariba, and Mobina laugh.

Mobina:
- Do you know what a race and a champion are?

P320:
- Yes.

Mobina:

- From this moment, we will all remain silent until we reach our destination. Anyone who speaks will be a loser.

Farhad:

- I agree. Just clarify my task before the start of the competition, where to go and what to get.

Fariba:

- First, go toward your butcher's shop, buy food and drinks for five people from the next restaurant, then go in any direction that P320 shows.

P320:

- There are no more than three of you. We do not eat anything.

Farhad:

- (laughing) Maybe if you eat, I will be hungry. What should I get now?

Mobina:

- Everything that you love, of course. We are supposed to eat Tahchin today.

Fariba:

- We will eat Tahchin tomorrow. Dear Farhad, get whatever you want.

Farhad:

- Well, let's go. Haven't you left anything?

Fariba:

- You said there is always recreational equipment in the car trunk.

Farhad:

- Apart from them?

Fariba:

- No, we didn't leave anything.

Farhad pressed the clutch, shifted the gear, started to move, and said,

- Oh God, my hope is in you.

Mobina:

- Shall we start the competition?

Everyone agreed, and the silence overwhelmed the place.

*****

After a while, the car turned off in front of a butchery. Farhad got out, went to the restaurant, ordered, came out, and went to the butchery. Mobina gave the pack to P300 as she held it and signaled him to go towards Farhad. P300 got out of the car with the pack in his hand and went to the butchery.

A few minutes later, Farhad and P300 came out wearing different clothes. Farhad went to the restaurant, pickup the food, and came to the car with P300. He signaled others to get out of the car and get in another car. P320 was shocked more than anyone else, but he got in the other car with others.

Farhad started the car, and after moving, he said,

- Sit tight. We need to leave the car at the right time.

A few moments later, suddenly, he quickly turned into the alleys, and after passing through some alleys, he entered a street.

After leaving the city, he entered a country road. Later, Farhad looked behind through the rearview mirror and said,

- The situation is not dangerous.

Fariba:

- Do we have any more pursuers?

Farhad:

- No, I'm not sure he was looking for us. I left it.

Mobina:

- (laughing) Dear uncle, you were James Bond, and we didn't know.

Farhad:

- (laughing) If I survive Miss Marple's mission, I will register for Formula One.

P300:

- P320, which way should we go?

P320:

- I am the champion of the competition. What is the prize?

Mobina:

- Do you have competitions in Souch planet?

P320:

- After the end of daily work, we all gather at the mouth of the cave to start running from there by counting one, two, and three. The first person whose hand touches the trunk of the Sishma tree will be the champion of the competition and the king of the story-telling banquet of Sishma. Now, what is my prize?

Mobina:

- After finding the leaf of Sishma, if the leaf sees fit, we will set up a banquet and listen to his storytelling, and then you will become the king of this banquet. It is better to find the Sishma leaf as soon as possible so that we know what decision it will make.

P300:

- Yes, that's the best decision. Now, P320, tell me which way to go.

*****

Then P320 directed, and Farhad moved the car. They reached the point where there was no way for the car to move.

Farhad:

- The car won't go further than this. If there is a long way left, we can try another route.

P320:

- No, it's nearby.

Farhad got off and said,

- We are going on foot. My dear sister and Mobina, stay here. We will come back.

Mobina got off with the others and said,

- I made all these plans to see this strange leaf. Mom and I will come too. I would like to hear a story from Sishma.

After everyone got off, Farhad locked the car door and said,

- I did not want you to walk. Now that you have decided to walk, go ahead.

P320 started walking, and others followed him. After passing some agricultural fields and a short hill, P320 sat on the ground and began to push aside some stones stacked irregularly on top of each other. They all came to his side and watched him.

P320 slowly raised a leaf, and a seed blew the soil covering them. He got up, showed them, and said,

- This is Sishma leaf and the red seed.

Mobina looked at the leaf and seed and said,

- What a beautiful leaf and a strange seed. I have never seen such a beautiful leaf before. Give it to me so I can look at it for a while and enjoy its sight. I will return it safely.

Then she took the leaf and red seed from P320.

Farhad looked at P300, pointed, and asked,
- Is it him?

P300 nodded and confirmed.

Farhad gave a signal, and they took P320 from both sides at once, with the help of P300.

Sishma leaf started to wail and said,
- Oh, Ir, help me. P300, why do you do this? What's going on here?

Mobina:
- So interesting, it talks.

P320:
- P300, what are you doing? Are you crazy?

P300:
- Dear Arash, you will understand soon.

P320:
- Who is Arash?

Farhad:
- Come on, apple juice.

Sishma leaf:
- What plan do you have in mind? Oh, Ir, save us. They deceived us.

Fariba opened the small bottle and gave it to Farhad. Farhad took the bottle and took it toward P320's lips.

Sishma leaf:

- P320, do not eat. Otherwise, you will be cursed by Ir.

P320 pressed his lips together hard and refused to eat.

Farhad:

- I would cut you into pieces. You have to eat. So, don't try in vain and eat like a human being.

P320 opened his mouth a little and said,

- We Ps that….

Farhad took advantage of the opportunity and forced the bottle into P320's mouth. He poured a sip of it into his mouth. P320 was forced to swallow while he was held tightly. P320 closed his eyes after several times and shook his head. He looked at P300 and asked,

- Pirooz, why did you hold me so tightly.

He looked at Farhad, Mobina, and Fariba and asked,

- Who are these? What are these tacky clothes?

While Farhad and Pirooz released him slowly, he looked at himself and said,

- And these clothes?

He put his hand on his head and continued,

- What a sweet and enjoyable seed it was. Where are the others? Ziba? Mahvash?

Pirooz:

- Dear Arash, be patient and think a little. Everything will be clear soon.

Arash went to a hill and climbed it. Others also followed him quickly, Pirooz looked around regretfully, and Arash was amazed.

Arash:

- That ruined minaret that can be seen from a distance is the minaret of….

Pirooz:

- Yes, it is the same, and where we have stood, a little more this side or that side, under our feet is Bab-e-Hormoz from the city of Gour.

Arash:

- It's not a pleasant joke.

Pirooz:

- There is no joke. Almost 800 years have passed and what you see in front of you are the ruins of the Gour city.

Arash sat on the ground, crossed his hands, and asked,

- 800 years? (Then he got up and continued) Ziba? Mahvash? Others?

Pirooz

- Don't worry, most probably they are in Souch now.

Arash:
-   Most Probably? You mean you don't know? How can I not worry as we trusted you?

Pirooz:
-   Be patient.

Arash:
-   How can I be patient when I have been separated from my friends? And you, who was our knower, does not know anything.

Pirooz pointed to the leaf in Mobina's hands and said,
-   Now, this leaf will tell everything.

Arash looked at the leaf and asked,
-   Are you crazy? How a leaf...

He suddenly fell silent, took another look at the leaf, which was like a human eye, and asked,
-   Isn't this the leaf of the same tree that was talking?

Pirooz:
-   Yes, it is the same, the Sishma leaf. (Then he turned to the leaf) Tell us what happened after eating those black seeds.

Sishma leaf didn't answer, and Pirooz asked again,
-   Didn't you hear what I said?

Farhad:
-   Maybe it doesn't know how to speak.

Mobina:
- No, dear Uncle, I heard its voice myself. It spoke.

Fariba:
- My daughter is telling the truth. I heard its voice too.

Farhad:
- Maybe you have a hallucination.

Mobina:
- Why?

Farhad:
- I don't know. Maybe it is due to the heat of the sun or hunger.

Mobina:
- I am sure there is no hallucination.

Farhad:
- Have you set up a court of inquisition in this hot summer under the bright sun?

Fariba:
- My brother is right. Let's go and sit under the shade of a tree. We will think later.

Mobina:
- Apart from all that, Uncle's meal time has passed, and he will get nervous gradually.

Farhad:

-   Oh, Mobina, I love you, as you have known your
    Uncle well.

Fariba:

-   Brother, tell her she has known herself well! Just like
    two peas in a pod, if the time for her food comes, she
    will eat all of us.

Arash:

-   That's a good idea. To be honest, I'm so hungry that
    I can't even walk. It feels like I have not eaten for
    years.

Then they began to leave.

Pirooz:

-   That is right, you have not eaten nor drunk for about
    800 years.

Arash:

-   How is that possible?

Pirooz:

-   Until now, you have been alive through light and air,
    and now you will need food like in the past.

*****

After a while, they sat in the shade of a stout tree and ate lunch.
Pirooz, who was busy examining the dishes while eating,
asked,

- What kind of dish is this? I have never seen anything like it. Why is it so thin and fat?

Mobina:
- Disposable dishes.

Arash:
- Does that mean you only use it once?

Fariba:
- We throw it away after using it. There is no need to wash it. It has made our work easier.

Pirooz:
- (thinking deeply) How many people live in this city?

Farhad:
- Eat your food. What do you have to do with the population of the city?

Mobina picked up her phone and, a little later, said,
- 417, 121 Tons.

Pirooz:
- Assume that one day all the people of the city use something like every three meals. How much volume of these do they throw on the ground in their surroundings? What do you people do with the earth? Once upon a time, outside the city of Gour was covered with trees and plants that were life-enhancing, and now....

Pirooz sighed and continued after a moment of silence.

- Keep on like this. One day you will be buried under the same things you throw out. When I came, I looked around in every corner, unusable items of various kinds littered everywhere, and there is no sign of the land that played a role of refreshment for Gour city before.

Mobina:

- It is not good to talk while eating.

Then she opened the soda bottle, poured a bit of soda, and drank it.

Arash:

- What was this boiling black thing that you were drinking it? Black wine?

Mobina:

- (laughing) No, it is soda pop, alcohol-free.

Arash:

- Does that mean it is not heady?

Mobina:

- No, it's just a food digester. (Then she poured it into a glass and held it towards) Try it.

Arash drank it little by little and said,

- Soda, it is interesting. Isn't it harmful like wine?

Fariba:

- Not like it, but it has disadvantages.

Pirooz:

- Then why do you drink it?

Farhad:

- Because it is delicious and cheerful.

Pirooz drank a little and said,

- From this point of view, you are right.

*****

After finishing the meal, Mobina got up, took a plastic garbage bag from the car's trunk, put all their garbage in it, and picked up some garbage that she saw around. She put the plastic garbage bag in the trunk of the car the returned to where she sat.

Mobina:

- If everyone cared about the environment and did not leave garbage, we would have a soulful nature.

Fariba:

- Exactly. The problem is these uncultured people who dispose of garbage carelessly. Otherwise, disposable containers are so good.

Mobina:

- But Uncle Pirooz, I think you are right. It is better not to use disposable containers. I have heard that they are carcinogenic.

Fariba:

- It is not a solution. Imagine that whenever we want to take away food from a restaurant, we give two pots to the owner of the restaurant and say, *"Five dishes of barberry rice with chicken, please."* We would be mocked.

Mobina:

- It's not a bad idea. When everyone does so, it won't be ridiculous. The owner of the restaurant will also be happy.

Fariba:

- Why?

Mobina:

- There would be no need to buy disposable dishes, and this means more profit.

Farhad:

- Don't argue about this issue. Disposable containers based on a herbal base will be in the market, and the spread of these oil-based products will be removed.

Arash:

- Is it possible? How do they make containers based on a herbal base?

Farhad:

- As they make containers based on oily base.

Arash:

- What is oil?

Mobina:

- Liquid, similar to mud. It existed in your time. Let me see. (She searched her phone and continued) Iranians used it for bituminizing their warships. In ancient Egypt and Iran, they knew the sources and used them.

Pirooz:

- Is bitumen called oil now?

Mobina:

- Thousands of new products are obtained from the same smelly sludge in the refineries. There is oil in most of the things you see around you, from the soles under our feet to the shoes and clothes we wear. Bitumen is only one of them that is mostly used in road construction.

Pirooz:

- It means it is the same bitumen that burned on our torches or bituminized the ships. Was it so valuable? These black roads are made from bitumen. My God, what a valuable element I had in my possession, and I was unable to understand it by researching it. I could have done many activities and didn't. I was wandering in Souch during my life and the reason

for this wandering... Bring the Sishma leaf. Anyway,
it should be responsible for this wandering.

Mobina opened her notebook, took out the Sishma leaf, closed
the notebook, put it on the ground, and placed the Sishma leaf
on it.

Fariba:
- Why has this leaf not dried? It is very interesting.

Mobina:
- Don't you notice the pale eye in its middle?

Farhad:
- Let's skip that eye. I think it looks like the leaf of a
plant that I have seen a lot.

Mobina:
- Yes, but what I saw was a few leaves stuck together.
This is not more than one.

Fariba:
- The leaf of what?

Mobina:
- I don't know what the leaf is. I have seen its picture
on several cars.

Farhad:
- Well done. That's right; it's the same, hempseed.

Pirooz:
- You're right. I hadn't noticed until now.

Arash:

- Let's go of it like everything is fine. We have another job, Mahvash, Ziba, and our friends. Have you forgotten?

Pirooz:

- Sishma leaf, tell us what happened after eating the black seed.

Sishma leaf did not reply.

Arash:

- Didn't you hear what he said?

Farhad hit the leaf a few times with his finger and said,
- Maybe it fell asleep.

Pirooz:

- No.

Mobina:

- How do you know?

Pirooz:

- It's not like when they sleep .One day, we went to Sishma's side together, and when we arrived, all its leaves were folded in half like closed books. I called it, but it did not answer. I was worried. I went closer and hit its trunk a few times. Suddenly, a branch threw me back. A few moments later, its leaves opened. Sishma sighed and said, *"Why did I sleep so much today? Because my wife talked so much last night and didn't let me sleep. This is how I knew he had fallen asleep."*

Arash:

- Hey, we are talking to you. Do you pretend that you are not able to hear? Tell us what happened after eating the black seeds.

The Sishma leaf did not answer again.

Farhad:

- Let's assume that someone comes by and sees that we have placed a leaf in the middle, and we ask him to answer. What would he think?

Mobina laughed and said,

- Nothing, we don't need to care about anyone.

Pirooz:

- It seems that there is no choice but to go to Souch.

Mobina:

- I don't think it is a wise idea.

Farhad:

- How, my dear?

Mobina:
- First, I am still not sure that those in Souch are their companions. Assuming they are, they would not know Pirooz and Arash, just like P320 did not recognize Pirooz at first.

Fariba:
- My daughter is right.

Arash:
- So, what should we do?

Farhad:

- Anyway, I will make the Sishma leaf talk. Hey, damnable leaf, I will peel you unless you talk like a human.

Fariba:
- Brother! First, this is not a person, then how do you want to peel it?

Farhad:
- I wanted to make it afraid so it could open its mouth. Anyway, what does it have to do with me?

Pirooz:
- That's right, it should be afraid. But what is it afraid of? What are plants afraid of?

Farhad:
- I got it, an axe. Bring an axe and cut it into pieces.

Mobina:
- Isn't the chain saw better?

Farhad:
- (laughing) Does such a small leaf need an axe? It can be cut by hand or fire.

Pirooz:
- That's what I wanted to say, fire!

Arash got up and said,
- I will look for flint in a short time and start the fire.

Farhad:
- Sit down. There is no need. We don't live in the mediaeval ages.

Then he put his hand in his pocket, took out a lighter, and lit it.

Mobina:
- Uncle! Lighter?

Farhad:
- My dear, it will be used for setting the fire and not for anything else. Be positive, girl.

Pirooz looked at it shockingly and said,
- Does it mean that a fire can be set so easily?

Mobina:
- This is also something derived from the same crude oil.

Fariba:
- Are you holding a class? Did you forget the Sishma leaf?

Farhad picked up the leaf and lit the lighter; he took it towards the leaf and said,
- Are you talking, or should I burn your lineage? One, two, Three.

Then he put the flame of the lighter under the leaf for a short moment. He stopped and continued,
- This is the last chance. This time, I will not show mercy. I will burn you, and then I will go to Souch with Arash and Pirooz by pressing a button then I will set the whole tree on fire. Mobina, show it the video of an explosion so that it understands that I am not joking.

Mobina:
- My dear, what should I search for?

Uncle:
- Write, "The explosion of the gas tanker at the gas station yesterday."

Mobina was searching her phone, and moments later, she showed the video to the Sishma leaf.

Farhad:

- Did you see it? I did so yesterday by pressing a button. You won't even have a chance to beg, let alone have someone to help you.

Mobina:

- Uncle, don't burn it. Show mercy to it.

Farhad:

- I should burn it so that it will be a lesson for others. (Then he lit the fire and started counting) One, two, three. (He put the flame of the lighter under the leaves.)

Sishma leaf:

- I got burned. Are you crazy? What evil have I done to you?

As soon as Farhad heard the voice of the leaf, he turned off the lighter, placed the leaf on Mobina's diary notebook, and said,

- Finally, it talked.

Sishma leaf:

- What does anything have to do with you that you meddled into everything concerning me and my kind friend Pirooz?

Pirooz:

- How am I your kind friend when you were silent until now?

Sishma leaf:
- I didn't want to talk to you in front of strangers.

Mobina:
- Why are you lying? You had already spoken. You do not remember? You told P320 not to eat, or he will be cursed by Ir.

Arash:
- Who is the P320?

Pirooz:
- You will understand soon.

Arash:
- Enough lying. Tell us what happened after eating those black seeds.

Farhad showed the lighter and said,
- Don't forget, if you lie, I will burn you.

Sishma leaf:
- There is no need for that lighter. I will tell you everything because my wife is interested in talking with you. I wanted to satisfy you with the taste of the pleasant seeds so that you stay in Souch and enjoy eating them forever. But after eating those seeds, a transformation occurred that I did not expect to occur. I realized that you had forgotten everything. You didn't even know your name. After some time, you took your name from P1 and Z1 to P730 and Z730. You even divided the Souch planet into two

equal parts. Mobina, Fariba, and Farhad know the rest.

Pirooz:

- I don't know why you decided to lie. Insisting on us eating the seeds at the same time has another meaning.

Farhad picked up the leaf and shouted,

- You lie?

Then he lit the lighter and said,

- It's no use. Let me set this lying leaf on fire so that it will serve as a lesson to other leaves.

Sishma leaf:

- Ah, Ir, help me. If he does this, there won't be any leaf left for me to learn a lesson. For the sake of God, free me from this, a lighter in the hands of a madman.

Mobina:

- My uncle is not crazy at all. This is the punishment for a liar. (And turned to her uncle), When it tells a lie, the eyes on the leaf become bolder. It is easy to tell that it is lying.

Pirooz:

- Really? You are so accurate.

Fariba:

- It's like you still don't realize what a big crime you have committed, a crime as great as 800 years.

Sishma leaf:

- Why do you add to it? 384 years.

Pirooz:

- Of course, turning the Souch year into Earth years is exactly 768 years, 3 months, and 27 days.

Arash:

- 800 years. What's the difference now, even one day? Misleading Gour people was a big mistake.

Pirooz:

- Tell me everything. Maybe we will forgive you.

Sishma leaf:

- After eating the black seeds, you had forgotten everything except one thing, that couples were always together. You knew you were connected but didn't understand the relationship.

Sishma leaf:

- No one spoke for a few days, but by testing the shadows, they found out that they couldn't stand in the shadows and were all moving out of the caves into the light. The first word that they said was, *"Who are we?"*

Mobina:

- Did they ask you?

Sishma leaf:

- No, they asked themselves. It was like they were thinking out loud. I regretted this incident and wanted to end this confusion. This time I talked to my wife before doing anything to avoid her grumbles in the future. I said to my wife, *"Let's let them go so that they can return to the city of Gour."* She replied, *"If you do so, I will never speak to you, and I will not send any more pollen towards you to cover your flowers. Your fruits will not be able to grow, and I know you enjoy seeing them so much."* I said, *"They don't even know what their names are."* She said, *"You name them yourself."* I said, *"All the names I have heard from Pirooz's words are not enough."* She said, *"I don't know, find a way."* I said, *"Let me keep as many as I have names for and return the rest."* She said, *"You have no right to return any of them, not even one."* I asked, *"But how can I name all these?"* She replied, *"As you count your seeds."* I asked, *"How?"* She answered, *"I don't know, Pirooz 1, Pirooz 2 until the end and in the same way Ziba. And now stop talking because I didn't sleep* last night." I said, *"It is difficult to do these things. What should I do?"* She did not answer. I discovered that she had fallen asleep. That's how I came about P1 and Z1 after thinking for a few days.

Farhad:

- So, you simply called and named them?

Sishma leaf:

- No, I was thinking about how to tell them their names and get them to accept it, which caused another problem.

Fariba:

- What was the problem?

Sishma leaf:

- Two more questions came to their mind, and they asked themselves out loud.

Pirooz:

- What questions?

Sishma leaf:

- Who made us and how? I examined different answers in my mind. To be honest, I was afraid of the other questions.

Mobina:

- Well, what did you finally do?

Sishma leaf:

- I concluded that I should force others to answer their questions and not speak.

Arash:

- And who was this other one?

Sishma:

- This was exactly the question I asked myself, and I thought about the answer for a while. I had to build a power beyond myself so that it would be easy to accept, but what power? There was nothing in Souch. At first, an imaginary creature living in the cave came up to my mind, but I was afraid that they would find a way and go inside the cave. It was not a good idea. Suddenly, I remembered Pirooz's words.

Pirooz:

- Which words?

Sishma leaf:

- Somewhere in the middle of your speech, you said that Ardeshir took Izadi's splendor and became the king of Iranshahr. I thought about this until I asked you one day.

Pirooz:

- Yes, I remember. You asked what Izadi's splendor was and why Ardeshir took it. And I answered, "*A sign of the kingdom that is granted by God to the chosen ones.*"

Sishma leaf:

- Yes, and I asked, "*Who is God?*" And you answered, "*The one who is in the sky. He made the Earth and us, and we worship him.*"

Pirooz:

- Yes, I said so.

Mobina:

- Well, what happened next?

Sishma leaf:

- That was the best idea. I had to make a powerful God and refer everything to him.

Fariba:

- Well, then?

Sishma leaf:

- The most powerful being, I used to cure my loneliness by talking to him, even though he never answered. But I knew very well that I needed him. Yes, there was no one better than him. Ir was the one who gave light and warmth to life. They believed him and my story easily.

Mobina:

- This is how you taught them to go to the cave, to burn one by one and in the morning after coming out, they should prostrate ten times as their chests touch the ground and respect him, is that right?

Sishma leaf:

- No, I thought a lot about how to say that until that event happened.

Arash:

- What happened?

Sishma leaf:

- One day, as I was watching them from above, I noticed a couple sitting on the stone at the mouth of the cave. I was curious about what they were going to do. After a while, they all passed out in front of me and remained there.

Farhad:

- Well then?

Sishma leaf:

- It was like they didn't intend to leave. Moments after the shadow arrived, they fell asleep as they sat. When it was completely dark, and I could not see them any longer, I noticed that they started to burn and had a dim and harmonic light.

Fariba:

- Why did they do that?

Sishma leaf:

- I don't know, maybe they were tired of going around Souch.

Pirooz:

- It is most probably for the same reason. I have experienced it.

Arash:

- What happened next?

Sishma leaf:

- I didn't sleep that night until morning; to be honest, I was more worried that flames would rise from them and burn the dry leaves of Savich, and then all of us would burn. As soon as they burnt, I saw two ten-year-old children sitting on a rock. After a while, others arrived and asked, *"Who are you, and where did you come from?"* I realized that those two children didn't have memories from before they were burnt. A quick thought crossed my mind; yes, this was the best way. I waited until they all came near me.

Mobina:

- What an idea!

Sishma leaf:

- Aren't you tired? I'm tired. I want to catch my breath.

Fariba:

- It's a good idea. Let's rest a little.

Farhad:

- If we continue like this, we will not be able to realize the reality until night.

Mobina:

- What's wrong with the night?

Farhad:

- Should we go home at night? Remember the case
agent?

Mobina:

- Don't worry. As soon as we get home and he sees us,
he will come by himself.

Farhad:

- Dinner and snacks?

Fariba:

- We will get something from the grain field in the
village.

Farhad:

- Does that mean we should stay here for the night?

Fariba:

- Do you know a better place? Let's go to Meimand[1]
side-track, next to the dam.

Pirooz:

- Has a dam been built in the middle of Meimand
road? Let's go. I am eager to see it.

Mobina:

- No way, we cannot go to Shiraz.

---

[1] Meimand: A town near shiraz, Famous with their rose water.

Arash:

- Shiraz? Where is Shiraz?

Mobina:

- A city that was established and formed after the recession of Istakhr and its abandonment. It is now the capital of the Fars province or the state of Pars.

Pirooz:

- Does it mean that Istakhr is also ruined?

Mobina:

- Most of the cities you know are now extinct. They have become a part of history.

Arash:

- The world I am in now is much more unknown and scarier than I thought. Until this moment, I would've never imagined this strange chariot, the types of equipment, or these strange clothes.

Pirooz:

- This city of Shiraz that you say is established beside Istakhr?

Mobina:

- No, about fifty kilometers or eight Parasangs1 you use to say instead of kilometer.

---

1 Parasang is a Persian ancient unit of distance and about four miles (six kilometers)

Fariba:

- Honey, if your history class is over, can you tell me why we can't go next to the dam?

Farhad replied,

- This is part of Miss Marple's plan.

Fariba:

- What does that mean?

Farhad:

- I need to know why the clothes of Pirooz and I changed. Why was our car changed?

Fariba:

- Well, why?

Farhad:

- (laughing) Now, the agent or the case agents have wandered around the Qal'eh Dokhtar to find me.

Fariba:

- Speak clearly, so I can understand what you are saying.

Mobina:

- My dear mom, I gave a piece of paper to my uncle in the yard and told him, *"Whatever I said about helping Pirooz, I was just joking. I have nothing to do with Pirooz. I found this paper among mom's clothes. Look, you will understand."*

Fariba:

- A piece of paper? Among my clothes? What are you saying?

Mobina:

- I had written on the paper that, most probably, tracing devices or microphones have been set in your clothes and Pirooz's. Mom and I have changed our clothes. You should also change your clothes. Now what you are doing is this, loudly and in a way that shows you are upset, say, *"I will do it, dear uncle, don't worry."* Uncle also said the same sentence that I had written. Then I gave him two more sheets on which I had written all the things we have to do.

Fariba:

- So, tell me, did you write these in the room? When I asked you, *"What did you write?"* You answered, *"It is a secret. You will understand soon."*

Mobina laughed, and Farhad said,

- After moving, it started with a contest of not speaking. I gave another paper to my brother Arash in a butchery, and he also read it without hesitation. We changed our clothes and then the car keys. Arash, according to Miss Marple's plan, closed the shop after we left while carrying Pirooz's previous clothes in the bag, moved towards the Qal'eh Dokhtar with my clothes and car. Without a doubt, he has hidden somewhere nearby.

Fariba:

- What are you saying? Why?

Farhad:

- Like me, he sent a text message to his wife and wrote that his phone was out of battery and they shouldn't be bothered if it turns off. Then, without a doubt, he turned off his phone like me, and now he has no entertainment for himself. Even worse, he is not even allowed to talk until night.

Farhad laughed, looked at Mobina and continued.

- Mobina, only God knows how long you have to seek the affection of Arash. I will lay the blame at your door, but then that's your own choice.

Mobina:

- Uncle Arash is the best uncle in the world. Just like you, he is attractive too.

Fariba:

- Miss Marple should learn from Mobina.

Pirooz:

- Who is Miss Marple?

Mobina:

- She is the main character in Agatha Christie's crime stories.

Arash:

- Agatha Christi?

Mobina:

-   The author of the story is English. He is not Iranian.

Fariba:

-   Let's skip these detective games. Where should we go?

Farhad:

-   My friend has a beautiful vacation cabin in this village. It's a pity that my phone is switched off. Otherwise, I would have arranged for it through a phone call.

Mobina:

-   Call with my phone.

Farhad:

-   His number?

Mobina:

-   Turn on your phone for a moment, get the number, and turn it off quickly.

Farhad:

-   Okay, Miss Marple.

Then she immediately did so, got up, and walked away while he was making a call on the phone.

Fariba:

-   (To Mobina) You told me to turn off your phone, so why is your phone on?

Mobina:

- Don't you remember that we register my SIM card
under the name of your cousin, Zhaleh? do not worry
we are done before they figure it out.

Farhad returned. He smiled and said,

- Get up and let's go. Cabin is all ours now.

Fariba:

- So, where is the cabin key?

Farhad:

- She told me where she hides the key. It's only 10
minits away from here. I have been there several
times before. It is a cozy place.

A few minutes later, after buying their necessities from the
village store, they sat on the platform in front of the small
building in the middle of the pleasant plain of flowers.

Farhad, as he was eating snacks like others, said,

- Well, break time is over. Put the Sishma leaf in the
middle so that we can continue the questioning.

Like before, Mobina put the Sishma leaf on her diary notebook.

Farhad:

- Did you catch your breath? Now go on.

Sishma leaf:

- What was I saying?

Pirooz:

- A quick thought crossed your mind. You waited until they all approached you, then?

Sishma leaf:

- I said I know. They all looked around. Someone asked loudly, *"Who knows?"* There was a heavy silence; I said again, *"I know."* Everyone's eyes turned towards me, and they gathered around as they hesitated. One asked, *"Who are you?"* I said, *"The Sishma tree, the most knowledgeable being from the Souch planet in the Ir system of Ann galaxy."* Someone asked, *"How do you know these things?"* I said, *"I am the same age as the Souch planet, and you have only been on this soil for a few days."* Someone asked, *"Who are we?"* Another asked, *"What are we doing here?"* I said, *"You have just been made by Ir, and you are not yet complete. The wind has brought the message of Ir to invite you to the Mehregan festival[1]."*

Mobina:

- Why celebration?

Sishma leaf:

- To be honest, I missed the celebration that Pirooz and Ziba held in the early days of their arrival in

---

[1] Mehregan festival is a Zoroastrian and Iranian festival celebrated to the yazata honor Mithra (Persian: Mehr), which is responsible for friendship, affection and love.

Souch. I had not seen such a pleasant rotation and much laughter and applause that were agreeable.

Pirooz:

-   Why Mehregan?

Sishma leaf:

-   This was the only name I remembered from Pirooz words.

Arash:

-   Well, what happened next?

Sishma leaf:

-   Someone asked, "*What is the festival of Mehregan?*" I said, "*Recently, two of you have reached perfection and are now famous.*" I showed them by my branch and continued, "*Open the way for them to approach.*" When they came close to me, I said, "*You should be proud of yourselves that you are the first ones to achieve development in Souch, and Ir has chosen a name for you. From now on, you are P1, and you are Z1. Now, everyone, celebrate this development. Stomp, laugh, and be happy because of this development.*" Someone asked, "*How should we do these things you said?*" I spent that day remembering and teaching the rhythmic movements that I learnt from Ziba and Pirooz. We spent the time celebrating, and when there was nothing left to do, I said, "*It is enough for today. Tomorrow, we will hold the Mehregan Festival again.*" Then I met the couple who had made the most effort to learn and said, "*You were chosen by Ir for your hard effort to reach the desired perfection. Stay here so I can tell you the message of Ir."* Someone said, *"So what about us?"* I said, *"Don't worry, your turn will come. Now worship Ir every day."* Someone asked, *"Who is this Ir you are talking about?"* I pointed at them with a branch and said, *"Just raise your head. His forgiveness and kindness are obvious. Have you not yet understood what will happen if he turns away from you for a moment? He is your lover. You should also love him and try to please him. Now follow him, for time is limited."* After they had all gone away, I showed the cave to the chosen couple and told them to go to the cave and sit on the stone at the cave's mouth and be patient. I told them they had an appointment with Ir and they shouldn't be afraid of the darkness because, after every darkness, the light will appear. *"Your victory over the fear of the darkness is similar to reaching the desired development, so don't hesitate and obey,"* I said.

Mobina:

-   So they agreed to go toward the cave so easily?

Fariba:

-   Mom, why won't they go? The promise of development and perfection seems attractive.

Mobina:

-   Does that mean they are not afraid of the darkness?

Pirooz:

- Don't you remember? Until now, they were fearless people of Gour.

Arash:

- You should have been there and seen with your own eyes how they had lost their lives to achieve freedom.

Farhad:

- Let the Sishma leaf continue. Otherwise, we will lose time and achieve nothing.

Pirooz:

- It is true what you say. (To the leaf) Well, what happened next?

Sishma leaf:

- Many days passed like this, and the further we went with the celebration of Mehregan for reaching perfection, the more magnificent the Ps and Zs became and the thirst of the remaining ones for evolution increased. Sometimes they would complain that it was not their turn. I was thinking of how to solve these complaints, and I couldn't find a more suitable solution than running. One day, I said to everyone, *"Today, just like the past days, this couple had been selected by Ir for their great efforts, but from tomorrow, Ir asks that after the morning meeting of those who have attained perfection, look at Ir and lay on the ground ten times with your chest and get up. Then the couples would hold hands together and count one, two, three, then run to me. Any couple who touches my trunk first will become the king of story-telling and, at the end of the day, will be perfected. So I began to tell stories I heard from Pirooz that day."*

Mobina:

- So interesting the race that P320 mentioned started like this. But one important point remains; the separation of Ps and Zs? High wall?

Sishma leaf:

- (sighed) I wish I had never started telling stories. Big trouble was forming. I used to tell stories every day and at night before going to bed because I was always enthusiastic about the events of that day. I was ignorant of the fact that this had caused me to start giving little attention to my wife. After a while, the ominous incident happened.

Fariba:

- What happened?

Sishma leaf:

- I remember that night exactly. It was the time for Pirooz and Ziba to be burned. I started to explain to my wife enthusiastically. She answered sharply and said, *"Stop. I don't want to hear anything. From now on, I will not speak to you, and I will not send any more pollen to you."* I said, *"Why? I did all these things for your pleasure."* She said, *"For me?"* She laughed loudly and said, "*I was just babbling. I said,* "*What happened?*" She said, "*What do you want to happen? You have taken possession of them on your own.*" I said, "*You are wrong.*" She said, "*There is only one way left for you.*" I asked, "*What way?*" She answered, "*Souch should be divided into two equal parts, half of Souch should be for me, and the other half should be yours.*" I said, "*What does that mean?*" She said, "*Just what you heard.*" I said, "*After all, they move under the light of Ir; they cannot stay in one half of Souch.*" She said, "*I don't understand these words. You created such a situation. Find a way yourself. Otherwise, as I said, I will not answer you from this moment. You Know me, there is no other way.*" From that moment on, no matter what I said and suggested, she gave no answer. I realized that I had no choice but to do what she wanted. I did not sleep that night until the morning. To be honest, I couldn't think of anyway. That night, I could only see the harmonious light from Pirooz and Ziba burning and the hope that burned inside me. The next day, the light of Ir lit up the stone of rendezvous where P300 and Z300 were born. Others arrived for the ceremony to respect Ir and then the competition. When P301 and Z301's hands touched my body the next day, I was full of great sadness. I was confused. I wanted to share Pirooz's potion, which had now dried up and turned into red and green seeds, among others, so that they could eat it and return to Gour. But this didn't solve my problem. Apart from that, I had found a strong attachment to their presence, which would make it impossible to forget them. That night, I decided they all burn and become children and the next day, I would start again, and this time I would not tell stories.

Farhad:

- So, you burned them all that night?

Fariba:

- Brother! Be patient; let it speak.

Sishma leaf:

- Someone shouted that *"Kind Sishma, where are you? Now is the time to tell a story."* I remember that day well. I told them a story about Ali Baba and the forty thieves of Baghdad. After the story, I shouted at everyone to be quiet, and then I closed my leaves and opened them after a few minutes. Then I said, *"A new order has been received by Ir. Soon, a big test will be held for the chosen couple and all of you on the Souch planet."* Someone asked, *"What kind of test?"* I said, *"A test of courage and silence."* Another asked, *"How?"* I said, *"Don't be afraid of the darkness and be quiet regardless of whatever you see. The test of your silence will start from now until the dawn of tomorrow. Do you understand?"* Most of them answered, *"Yes."* I said, *"Many of you now have failed this test. This time, all the wrongdoers are forgiven, but be careful not to repeat your mistakes because there will be no forgiveness. The test of silence is very difficult, have you noticed?”* This time, everyone fell silent. I said, *“Well done to you, the chosen ones and the fearless ones of Souch. Now everyone should be seated silently.”* An hour later, I said, *“Well done to you, the chosen ones of Ir. Now the chosen couple, stand up.”* I showed them the cave with my branch and said, *“Go in search of Ir. Go inside the cave, sit quietly in the middle of the cave, and close your eyes. Do not be afraid that the test of courage has already started, and Ir is the guardian of chosen ones.”* The chosen couple moved, and I saw them enter the cave. After a while, seeing the pale light that could be seen from the opening of the cave, I turned to the others and said, *“But you have an easier task. When I say get up and go to the cave, enter the cave, and when you enter, you will see the chosen couple bright and luminous; don't be afraid and don't worry. Sit around them in such a way that you all see the chosen couple. You must see them and be silent until morning. Tomorrow morning, all of you leave the cave. I wish everyone success with this test, Ir will help you. Get up now and fight your inner fears.”*

Mobina:

-   Does that mean they all left?

Fariba:

-   I don't think so.

Farhad:

- Have they been maddened to leave?

Arash:

- It is not unlikely that all of them have gone. I have seen their fearlessness.

Pirooz:

- (To leaf) What happened in the end?

Sishma leaf:

- A great concern bothered me from inside; the fear of their disobedience and rebellion. Shockingly, I saw with my eyes that they had all entered the cave.
It is difficult for me to believe they had such courage. That night, I didn't sleep until morning. Fear had weakened me. One of these 730 couples who were burning could come to me and take revenge. Another question that I had not thought about bothered me; what happened to the children after being burned? Sometimes I dreamed people in the process of burning, who ran towards me as they were screaming, and sometimes I see nightmares like petite and husky children who were ruining Souch without noticing me. They cut Savich bushes into pieces. They were pointing at my leaves and throwing stones at them. That night, until the morning, I suffered more than I had my entire life.

Mobina:

- Tell me, in the morning, what happened?

Sishma leaf:

- In the morning, while I was very worried, I saw all of them come out of the cave. Contrary to my nightmares, others who had gone into the cave after the chosen couple had not burned. They held a ceremony to respect Ir. After seeing the ceremony, I calmed down a little. Then they all ran towards me. I didn't know what would happen after they arrived and what I should say. The first couple whose hand touched my trunk held the Mehregan celebration of P301 and Z301 more magnificently than before. They were happy as they wanted to pass the test very well. They had come out of the cave proudly, and I had forgotten the burning sensation in my eyes, which was due to insomnia two nights ago. After the celebration, they all sat around me and were ready to hear the story when suddenly P300, which is a child now, asked, *"Why did those two ones burn the night before? Why should I love Z300 and stay with her forever?"* A wave of tremor shivered all my leaves, the fear of more questions was deadly. I fell silent for a moment and thought about the answer. I sighed and said, *"Why has Ir assigned such a thing? It is an unforgivable mistake. Ir helps us. Only he knows that from the moment I was informed of the arrival of the great test. I whispered to Ir so that you could come out of it proudly. I haven't slept for two days and nights, and I've been whispering to Ir, is this my reward? Today I won't tell any stories, and you will have the test again like the day before. I will close my eyes to visit Ir in my dream. Maybe I could convince him to forgive this big mistake. The test of your silence will start from now. Then I closed my eyes and slept."*

Fariba:

- What did he ask that you treated him so harshly?

Mobina:

- There must have been another reason.

Pirooz:

- By being wise, he has nipped all the questions in the bud so that no one would be able to ask.

Arash:

- Indeed, he is experienced.

Farhad, who had been listening while he made preparations for the barbecue and had lit a small fire in the broiler to prepare the coals, said as he smiled,

- "He was sleepy. He excused these questions; maybe a combination of both. What happened next?"

Sishma leaf:

- The next day, after holding the Mehregan celebration of P302 and Z302, I told them a short story. After that, I sighed and said, *"But kind Ir will forgive this big mistake on the condition that you fulfill his request."* Someone asked, *"What does he want?"* I answered, *"Now, it is necessary for all Zs and also the other Zs who will come in the future to migrate towards my wife and all the Ps and other Ps who will come in the future stay here.*" They all looked at me surprisingly, and none of them showed any reaction. Little by little, I could hear whispers. I was afraid of their disobedience, and there was nothing left for me but fear. Suddenly, the Ir was put out, and everyone was afraid. I was full of joy.

Mobina:
- Why were you happy?

Sishma leaf:
- The yearly event I was waiting for happened, and according to my plan, they were all scared.

Mobina:
- Does this mean Ir will be put out every year?

Sishma leaf:
- Yes, on the same day and at the same time. As usual, I immediately shouted, *"Don't be afraid and don't worry, Ir will come back soon. After a while, the Ir lit up again"*, and I said loudly, *"This was just a little warning for all those who had doubts in their hearts. If you do not respond to his wishes, he will turn his eyes away and remain silent until all of you fade away. Then he will build new Ps and Zs that will be obedient and concerned about reaching perfection."* I kept silent for a while so that fear spreading among them. P1 asked as his voice was trembling, *"What should we do now to make Ir happy?"* I said, *"As I said, I count to 10. After that, all of Zs and the other*

Zs who will come in the future should move and migrate towards my wife." Then I started counting. I had not yet reached number 5 when most of them started to leave. After saying 10, they were all leaving. Ps and the other Ps who would come in the future were slowly going behind them. I shouted, "*Hey, Ps, that's enough. Everyone, come back!*" All of them returned. P303, whose turn it was to be burned that night, asked, "*When will this separation end?*" I said, "*Don't worry, Ir is kind and surely has a reason for this. This separation will end whenever he recommends.*"

Pirooz:

- Woe to me for bringing all these people to reach an empty desire. It is hard for me to believe this is the same Sishma tree.

Fariba:

- How did your heart let you separate them? You should have shown mercy to them.

Mobina:

- Hardhearted.

Arash:

- Apart from its hard-heartedness, its flaws are so visible.

Sishma leaf:

- I know you are right. I had this dream myself that I would satisfy my wife as soon as possible so that they could be together again. I liked them more when they stayed with each other.

Farhad:

- Well, is your wife finally satisfied?

Mobina:

- What kind of question is this, dear uncle? It is clear that the answer is no. Don't you remember P300 said we have nothing to do with each other? (To leaf) You must have forced them to build a high wall later, right?

Sishma leaf:

- No, I was still hoping for Zs to come back.

Fariba:

- So, how was the wall built?

Sishma leaf yawned and said,

- Now, it's time for me to sleep. I will tell you tomorrow.

Pirooz:

- We didn't come here to see you dream.

Arash:

- Forget about sleep, time is short, and many things are left unsaid.

Farhad:

- The case agent will find us soon, You don't have time to sleep.

Sishma leaf:

- Well, they find us then.

Mobina:

- Do you think that if the officers find you, it will end with these simple questions? It will be a disaster that you'll wish to be burned a thousand times.

Sishma leaf:

- Why?

Fariba:

- A leaf that talks, the least trouble that will happen to you will be successive tests for identifying the elements that have formed you.

Mobina:

- This means that you will stay on Earth forever, or you can return to Souch with Arash and Pirooz and continue living.

Farhad took the leaf, brought it near the broiler, and said,

- Don't bother yourself about the chicken I am craving, Leaf Kebab.

Sishma leaf:

- Farhad has gone crazy again. Bring me back. I will not sleep.

Farhad returned the leaf and said,

- Well done. Now you have become a wise Sishma leaf. Now, tell me about that wall that my sister asked about.

Sishma leaf:

- As my wife had seen it from above for a few days, I had told her and said every night she should send the Zs to their cave, and in the morning, after coming out, they would respect Ir and run to her. They used to hold the Mehregan celebration, and my wife would tell them stories. But little by little, some of the Zs came near the border early in the morning and looked at Ps and me out of longing. I had fewer problems. I was engaging the Ps in stories excitedly that they didn't have a chance to think about the Zs. These regretful looks of Zs made my job of pleasing my wife every day difficult, to the point where she insisted on building a wall, and I accepted hesitantly. After the Mehregan celebration of P534, I shouted and said to the Ps, *"Woe to these Zs."* P27 asked, *"What happened?"* I said, *"They have committed an unforgivable sin and will be cursed by Ir soon."* P256 asked, *"What kind of sin?"* I said, *"I don't know properly. Ir asked me to tell you to take action to save yourself and build a wall on the designated border as soon as possible so that you will not be cursed like them. Otherwise, you will be destroyed with them."* P365 asked, *"What should we do if the curse of Ir comes before the wall is completed?"* I said, *"Don't worry. As long as Ir sees your efforts for building a wall, he won't curse you."* P463 asked,

"Does this mean we have to build a wall every day until night? That it is agonizing." I said, *"No, from tomorrow morning, after leaving the cave, respect Ir then start building a wall from the back of the cave on the designated border to the right until the middle of the day."* Then, everyone gathers in front of the cave. The competition holds, then we celebrate and after that, tell stories. The night will be like the past. Whoever is his turn will burn gloriously and give his light to others so they will live. Then I started telling stories every day.

Farhad:

- So, the wall was built only by Ps?

Sishma leaf:

- No, I told all the words to my wife that night, and she also said the same things about the Ps and forced the Zs to start building a wall out of fear of the curse that is going to befall the Ps. So, Ps were arranged on one side and Zs on the other.

Pirooz:

- No one asked about the curse after the completion of the wall?

Sishma leaf:

- Before they raised any questions, one day after starting the daily work that had been started after the completion of the wall, I shouted, *"Everyone, gather and come to me."* After they all came, I happily said,

"Today is the day of forgiveness. The order has been received to stop working today. Until the end of the night, be happy and dance in the celebration of forgiveness. Kind Ir saw Zs trying to build a wall. After being assured that the Zs will build a wall to protect you from the flame of their curse, he has forgiven their fault because of this good deed. Now, all of you should celebrate and sing the song of the kindness of Ir." My wife said the same about the Ps and celebrated the forgiveness too.

Mobina:

- The poor fox only took a cheese mold from the crow. They didn't give him any respect. The Sishma leaf should hold a training class for foxes as soon as possible.[1]

Fariba:

- (to Sishma leaf) How did you know they should not eat your leaf?

Sishma leaf:

- P365 was troublesome from the very beginning.

Arash:

- What did he do?

Sishma leaf:

- I had seen him trying the taste of fresh Savich leaves many times. I knew that one day he would try the

---

[1] In Iran, the fox is a symbol manipulation. (Translator)

taste of my leaf too. I didn't pay much attention. To be honest, I wanted to know what would happen after eating my leaf.

Mobina:
- Well, when did he eat it?

Sishma leaf:
- It was in the third year of their presence in Souch. One evening, earlier than usual, I said, *"Go now and be quiet. I am tired and need to rest."* After a few moments, I understood that P365 sat and entertained himself with something. I noticed that he had a plan in his head. I pretended to be sleeping then I felt the warmth of his hand on one of my leaves. I could have stopped him, but I preferred him to pick the leaf and eat it. A few moments later, I opened my eyes, and P365's muscles were getting bigger. At first, he was very scared, but after a while, he picked up a stone that he had not been able to lift before and threw it to one side. He fisted his two hands and looked at his arms. After a few moments, he laughed loudly. Suddenly, he realized that he was in the shadow of Ir's dusk. First, he took a few short steps towards the light, but he stopped and eyed himself amazingly. He took a deep breath. The shadow had not influenced him. He realized that he didn't need light any longer.

Farhad interrupted Sishma's words and said,
- Eat it before it gets cold.

Then he put all the grilled chicken skewers on the table. He sat and said,

-   Well, what happened next?

Sishma leaf:

-   A few minutes later, P365 looked at his stomach, put his hand on it, and pressed it a little. He experienced the feeling of hunger for the first time. He looked at me and came towards me. I was afraid that he would start eating my leaves. I had already defended myself when he suddenly put his hand on his mouth and nose, and some strange sounds came out of his mouth. Then he went back.

Mobina:

-   What kind of sound?

Sishma leaf:

-   I don't know. Whenever he came near me, this would happen, and he would immediately return.

Pirooz, who was eating, said,

-   Most probably, he vomited after smelling Sishma or its leaves.

Mobina, who wanted to put a morsel in her mouth, waited for a moment and asked,

-    Vomiting?

Arash:

-   It is a sign of poisoning or pregnant women.

Farhad:

- Well, say vomit.

Fariba:

- Farhad! We are eating.

Farhad:

- Let's skip that.

He looked at the leaf and asked,

- What happened next?

Sishma leaf:

- He went toward the Savich bushes and tried their leaves. He loved their taste and began to eat fresh Savich leaves enthusiastically. After a while, in harmony with the darkness on this side of the Souch planet, his eyes were closed for the first time, and he fell asleep under the bushes as drizzle fell softly on the ground. A little later, I also fell asleep. It was still not dawn when I woke up to a strange sound. I heard the sound of P365's short laugh. I saw he had sat on his feet, and something had come out of his body. Again, I heard the first sound and then P365's short laugh.

Farhad:

- I did not understand correctly. What has he been doing?

Pirooz:

- It is most probable that he was defecating, and that sound was related to the sound of his stomach passing wind.

Fariba:

- Please just let us eat in peace.

Farhad:

- (laughing) He voided for the first time, which was attractive and funny to him.

Arash:

- (to the leaf) What happened after that?

Sishma leaf:

- P365 got up, looked at what had come out of his body, and laughed. Then he shook his clothes, went toward another shrub, and started eating fresh Savich leaves.

An hour later, the Ps came out of the cave, and after respecting Ir, they held a celebration.

Mobina:

- Didn't they celebrate after the competition?

Sishma leaf:

- After leaving Ps, the celebration was not pleasant for me like before. I still long for those first days. Anyway, the competition had changed, and only some of the Ps were running to be the king of my storytelling. Their burning was predetermined, and they burned in order. After the celebration, they started doing their daily tasks. They were picking the extra Savich branches, stepping on the dry branches, and throwing them on the feet of the shrubs. Suddenly, P712 said, *"What is this? What a bad smell."* Soon, they all gathered around him in astonishment. They were checking the new product of P365. P300 spattered some dirt on him and said, *"Now, do your daily work."* We will ask Sishma while he is telling a story. A few moments later, after seeing P365, P516 asked him, *"Where were you in the cave last night as I didn't see you?"* P365 laughed and said, *"I wasn't there."* Then he started eating fresh Savich leaves. P516 said: *"What are you doing?"* P365 then said: *"It has nothing to do with you."* P516 went towards him to stop him, and then P365 pushed him. P516 was thrown back and fell to the ground. Soon, they all gathered around P365 and realized that he had changed. A few who considered themselves more powerful than others tried to stop P365, but it was useless; with a small movement, they were thrown back. They fell to the ground, and P365 laughed loudly. P300 said, *"We will ask Sishma if he knows."* Then they all moved towards me. I thought about the answer until they arrived. As soon as they were all in front of me, I said, *"I know what you want to ask. P365 has an incurable disease. What P300 spattered soil on it has been removed from the P365's body."* P300 asked, *"What *is an incurable disease?" I said, "Something that leads to death." P300, "Why did he come down with it?" I said, "An unforgivable mistake has been committed. Don't ask him anything or demand anything." P300 then asked, "Does that mean we should abandon him to be destroyed? This is not good. He is our friend and brother." I said, "The only thing you can do is to stretch your hand toward Ir every day after the ceremony of respecting Ir and ask Ir to forgive him. Ir will forgive him if he wants. Now, go and move away from him and do your daily work."*

Farhad:

- (laughing) This Sishma is a wonder plant. Whenever it didn't know what to do, it blamed everything on poor Ir and made gullible Ps pray to be entertained.

Arash:

- That's why I say he is adept pol.

Mobina:

- What does an adept pol mean?

Fariba:

- Skilled politician.

Pirooz:

- (to the leaf) How did you find the cure?

Sishma leaf:
- After a few days, I saw P365 lifting heavy stones. He used to throw them toward the wall and laugh. I didn't understand what was in his mind, but I think he wanted to ruin the wall and go towards the Zs.

Mobina:
- Did he ruin the wall and go toward the Zs?

Sishma leaf:
- No, there was one stone in all the planets that differed from other stones. Its appearance was glossy, with two relatively large holes in which rain drizzles accumulated at night. P365 went towards it and looked at me, then he looked at the stone and laughed loudly. He picked up the stone and came towards me. I couldn't see because of worry. Most probably, he wanted to throw the stone at me. I wanted to shout and call Ps to help me when he suddenly stopped. He drank the water inside the stone. It didn't take long before he fell to the ground and his eyes were closed. After a while, P365's eyes were opened. He got up from the dirt, looked around, then at the stone and said, *"Why is this stone here in the middle of the road?"* Then he bent down and tried to move the stone. He moved it a little, got up, and shouted, *"My good friend, P300, where are you? Come on. I need your help."* P300, who had heard his voice, approached and asked hesitantly, *"What do you want?"* P365 said: *"Help me to move this stone from the middle of the road."* P300 looked at

P365 shockingly, and then he turned to look at me. I told him, *"Don't worry, Ir is generous and kind."* As P300 was slowly approaching, I wanted to see the stone from a close distance; I said, *"Help me and deliver the stone to me."* As they held both sides of the stone and came towards me, I felt all my strength and power weaker. I said slowly, *"Come back."* Then they went back a little. I said, *"Put it on the ground so, I can ask Ir about it."* I closed my eyes and thought of what I would do if Pirooz or someone else discovered that this stone destroyed my power. A thought came to my mind. I opened my eyes and said, *"Ir has ordered to cut it in half now."* I was hoping that its power would disappear after the stone was halved. It took a while for them to break the stone. After the stone was broken, I said, *"P300, take one half and come to me."* P300 did so. I noticed the power of the stone had decreased, but it had not disappeared. I said, *"It is enough."* After he went back, I said, *"Put the stone on the ground and wait."* Then I closed my eyes and thought. Less than an hour passed before I opened my eyes and said, *"P300 come closer."* P300 came and did whatever I said. Then I said, *"Get up."* P300 got up and asked, *"Why are you doing that?"* I said, *"Now, wherever you are, I will see by your eyes and hear by your ears, and I will talk with you."* P300 asked, *"Why?"* I said, *"On behalf of the beloved of our hearts, Ir, you have been chosen to carry out a mission that will make everyone honored."* He asked, *"What is your mission?"* I gave him two red and green seeds and said, *"Hide the red seed in your clothes, and I will tell you what to do at the right time. Now, go to P365 and give him the green seed. Open the turban of your head and put it on the ground. Break a piece of his half stone and put it in your turban. With the help of P365, tie the turban to yourself in a way that the stone does not fall."* And P300 did so.

Mobina:

-   Ur-ra-nium stone?

Sishma leaf:

-   The same polished stone that had two holes and that I said to break in half. It needed a name, so I named it.

Mobina:

-   Well then?

Sishma leaf:

-   I said to P300, *"Now lie on your back to the ground."* P300 asked, *"What are these things for?"* I said, *"You will understand soon."* I said to P365, *"Put the green seed in his mouth,"* and he did so. I said to P300, *"Chew the seed and eat it."* A few moments later, P300 closed his eyes. He turned into a green light and disappeared. P365 was scared. I told him, *"Don't worry, P300 will return soon. I stay with him. Do not tell anyone about this until he returns."* When P300 opened his eyes, he saw himself in a ruin. I said to him, *"Get up and open your turban and easily take the stone somewhere."* P300 asked, *"Where am I? How scary is this place?"* I said, *"Don't be afraid of anything. Ir is your guard, and I stay with you. Now, get up and move to the right side."* For an hour, we passed through colorful trees and shrubs along with P300 until I saw a small hole in the ground that was the same size as the stone. I said to P300, *"Take the stone out of the turban, put it in the hole, and cover it with soil."* P300 did so, then he got up, shook his turban, and wrapped it around his head. I said to him, *"Our work is done. Now take out the red seed and eat it so that we can return to Souch together. Half of your mission is over. Ir has ordered you to come back here and complete the mission."* P300 said sadly, *"There is no red seed in my clothes."* I said, *"What does that mean?"* He said, *"I had left it here, but it is not there. What should we do now?"* I said, *"Don't worry."* I kept silent and said, *"Go to the hidden library."* He said, *"What is a hidden library?"* It was useless. I said, *"Forget it. Go back the same way you came and look at the soil. Even though I cared about it, I know it didn't fall on the way. But still, search the soil on the way back for the red seed."* We were returning and searching when a voice said, *"Peace be upon you, young man. What are you looking for among the trees and bushes?"* P300 answered helplessly, *"Hello, I'm looking for a red seed to eat and return to Souch."* The voice said, *"What are you saying?"* P300 raised his head and saw someone who looked like himself with white hair holding a rope and pulling something behind.

Then he got a little scared and asked, *"Who are you? What is it that you are pulling?"* He laughed and said, *"Do you want to pretend that you have never seen a donkey? You look like a witty young man. I am an old man from Kooshk, and now, I am returning from the garden toward Kooshk. Who are you?"* P300 was staring at what was behind the old man and did not answer. Old man said, *"This tongue-tied is as old as I am and cannot carry the saddlebag, I placed on it. Inside the saddlebag is some fruit that I will take to Kooshk to be sold."* P300 said, *"The name of this is tongue-tied?"* Old man: *"It is a donkey, and because it does not speak, we say that it is tongue-tied."* He was silent for a moment and continued. *"Are you okay? Are you hungry?"* P300: *"Who is hungry?"* The old man looked at P300 shockingly and said, *"It's like the sun has hit your head, and your mind has been lost."* Then he put his hand inside the saddlebag, took out something, and said, *"Take this apple and eat it so you won't die of hunger."* Then he forcibly put the apple in P300's hands and pulled the donkey; they moved and turned away. P300 looked at the old man and his donkey as they were moving. Then, he looked at the apple and took it toward his mouth involuntarily. I said, *"Wait. First, find the red seed to return to Souch, then try the apple."* We went back and searched the path to the place where he had landed. A red seed had fallen right there. He picked up the seed on the ground. A voice came. *"Hey, young man, what are you doing on the ruins of Bab-e-Hormoz from the city of Gour?"* I told P300 to eat the seeds quickly in order not to be caught. P300 started eating seeds. When P300 opened his eyes, he was in Souch. He got up, looked at the apple in his hand, and started eating until there was no trace of the apple left. P300 put a hand on his head and then looked around and shouted, *"Arash! Ziba! Mahvash! Where are you?"* Then he shouted, *"The fearless ones of Gour! Where are you?"* When he saw me and came toward me, I had a short time to think. I threw a black seed on the ground, and as soon as he arrived, he asked, *"Where are the others?"* I said, *"Look, the seed has fallen from your hand and you are left behind by others. Hurry and eat as long as there is time. Otherwise, forever here, you will be alone."* Pirooz took the seed quickly, peeled the skin, and ate it. I breathed a sigh of relief. A few moments later, P300 said, *"The mission has been successfully carried out. Now, if you permit, I will go to the cave before it gets dark."* I said, *"Ir will protect you. Go to the cave quickly as others worry about you."*

Pirooz:

-   So, you tricked me again, and I came down?

Sishma leaf:

-   I had no other choice.

Mobina:

- P300 was looking for uranium. They mean the same thing. Uranium?

Sishma leaf:

- Yes. Then P300 went behind someone who looked like P301 when he was changing his clothes. He asked P300, "*You didn't tell me what the story of the filming was about.*" P300 answered with my help, "*It is the story of someone who came from many years ago, and now he is looking for a uranium stone hidden in a hole many years ago.*" He asked, "*Do you mean uranium stone?*" P300 answered, "*Yes.*" I don't know why, but I liked this name more and told P300 to call it Uranium from then on.

Mobina:

- You said a piece of that stone; what was it like?

Sishma leaf:

- A polished and somewhat black stone, with relatively large holes on it, on one side of that which it was broken and split in half.

Mobina:

- (laughing) It is the characteristic of a stone based on what I heard. My father's grandmother, or the same Bibi, has used it as a , and now it has remained under the stairs of the house because of its beauty.

Fariba:

-   That is the one the officers took with them to check.
    Thank God that it's not uranium.

Farhad looked at the leaf and asked,

-   How was P300 supposed to get its extract?

Sishma leaf:

-   It was enough to pour some water into the hole of the
    stone and bring it with him after an hour to give to
    P365 and P730 so that they can return to their
    previous state. Now, we can look for another piece
    of stone that P300 brought the next day and hide it
    in another corner. Then we return to Souch with
    some water, and everything will be as before.

Pirooz:

-   (Voice dripping with sarcasm) And I will be P300
    again, Arash turns into P320, and the mission is done
    happily.

Arash:

-   I have never heard a more shameful word than this.
    Indeed, this leaf is so arrogant.

Farhad

-   (to the leaf) Where did you hide the other piece of
    stone?

Sishma leaf:

-   Somewhere near an elate pile of stones in the middle
    of the ruins of Gour.

Fariba:

- It says the minaret of Gour city.

Farhad:

- (laughing) That's all. All we need is to dig there and stay in prison forever for the crime of treasure finding.

Pirooz turned to Sishma and asked,

- What else did you not say?

Sishma leaf:

- I think I have said everything.

Mobina:

- You were one who always sat on their foreheads in the same Souch. How did you separate yourself from your branch and join P300?

Sishma leaf:

- I used to see the earth in a blurred state from Souch. I wanted to go with the P300 to see it closely.

Farhad:

- So, why had you been hidden?

Sishma leaf:

- I don't know why. As soon as I saw the large volumes, I observed relatively large areas. I realized that that area was Firoozabad. I was suddenly afraid. After seeing the plow and chariot, I realized how ignorant I was. Then I decided to hide until my ignorance left. Do not be a byword for P300 or other humans. I still don't know what that plow and chariot were.

Mobina:

- Tractor.

Pirooz turned to Sishma and asked again,

- What else have you not said?

Sishma leaf:

- It is not worth mentioning any more events. I have said everything necessary until now so that we can carry out the mission of P300 with the help of each other.

Farhad got up angrily, took the leaf, and threw it on the broiler's charcoals.

Sishma leaf:

- (moaning) Oh, I burned. Oh, Farhad, you are crazy. Oh, I b…u…r….n…e…d….

Then Sishma leaf turned into ashes.

Pirooz, who stood up to take the leaf, then realized that it was useless. He looked at the burning leaf with only compassion and regret and then asked,

- Farhad, why did you do that?

Farhad:

- I was waiting for it to finish its words before making it pay for its deceit.

Arash:

- It was a nice job. My pain got better a little.

Farhad:

- If I go along with you to Souch, I will also burn the tree so that the roots of lies and deceit will be removed.

Pirooz:

- But no one is going to accompany us. Mobina has one seed, which belongs to me, and the other seed in front of Arash belongs to him.

Farhad:

- It is easy for you to go to the hidden library. Make a potion and bring it.

Pirooz:

- (laughing) After 800 years? Even if termites have been jobless, they will not be found easily. It will take months, and now our companions are waiting for their release from the prison of Souch. We must return as soon as possible. Mobina, would you give me the red seed?

Mobina:

- But you need to come to our house and leave there without the knowledge of the agent officer. Otherwise, the three of us will be imprisoned for the rest of our lives because of the crime of taking you far away.

Arash:

- So, get up to go early.

Fariba looked at her watch and said,

- Let's sleep here tonight. We'll leave early in the morning.

Pirooz:

- Arash and I don't have time to stay. We have missed Ziba and Mahvash for 800 years. The fearless people of Gour are waiting for their release.

Fariba got up and said,

- Let's go soon.

Pirooz said while he was leaving,

- Woe to me! Farhad, why did you rush and burn the leaf? He talked about all the couples, but he didn't say anything about the little prince or Shapoor.

Mobina:

- It is useless to regret. I am sure that other questions will come to your mind. Ask the tree in the Souch.

*****

After a while, they all got in the car and moved towards the city.

Mobina:

- Uncle Pirooz, you didn't tell us anything about the successor of Ardeshir to Mongols' Holakoo Khan. You didn't tell us about the events of nearly a thousand years. I have thousands of unanswered questions. Would you come back?

Pirooz:

- I will return soon with Ziba. You also have not shown me the way to understand the countless questions, and you promised to help.

*****

After a while, they were all at the house, and the case agent asked Farhad,

- Why did you change your clothes and car?

Farhad:

- You hadn't said that we should not change.

Officer:

- Why was your phone and also your brother and sister's phone turned off?

Farhad:

- It didn't charge and turned off. What happened now? What do you and these two people have to do with us at all? Take them and ask them to take the paraphernalia you left at the house.

Pirooz and Arash started eating red seeds.

Mobina:

- Uncle Pirooz, I will wait for you.

A few moments later, their eyes were closed, and they fell to the ground. They turned into a red light and disappeared. The case agent was surprised. He ran like a deer caught in headlights in the place and was thinking about what he had seen.

Mobina:

- Oh no, apple extract they forget to take it. They rushed…

*****

The end of the first book.

Persian Ethion of Sishma

Other Books Worth to Read

How to Access Kidsocado Publishing House